THE KEEPING KIND

KILKENNY CHRONICLES, BOOK 1

KALLIE CLARKE

BLACK

www.BlackInkRomance.com

Cover design by Corey Majeau at Majeau Designs.

ISBN: 978-0-9865192-3-9

Created with Vellum

For K, K, and K…my life. My heart.

CHAPTER 1

"Hey! You can't drive. We've been drinking all night."

"Indeed, I can." Cassie Kennedy dug in her handbag for keys. "While you two were knocking it back, I was drinking water," she said.

"Who stays sober at their own hen doo?" Siobhan O'Mara, Cassie's oldest friend, asked.

"I read in one of those posh wedding magazines it was bad for the complexion," she said.

"So, you're telling me we're the unlucky bitches who'll have hangovers tomorrow." Siobhan hooked her thumb back and forth between herself and their other friend, Scarlett Shea.

"Looks like it." Cassie grinned, still fishing for her keys.

"Wouldn't be the first time." Scarlett stumbled over nothing in the parking lot.

"That's okay. My hangover lasts a day—your ball and chain is forever." Siobhan stuck her tongue out, reaching for Scarlett's hand to steady her friend.

Cassie fought the urge to take offence, but there was

deeper meaning in Siobhan's words. As the by-product of a tumultuous marriage with more domestic disputes to count, Siobhan had an unhealthy disrespect for marriage and commitment and one rule which she lived by: love 'em and leave 'em—and she was damn good at it.

"Aha!" Finally producing her keys, she clicked the button, but Siobhan's loud voice drowned out the soft thud of the shifting locks.

"What the hell?"

Startled, she opened the driver's door to see what Siobhan was yelling about.

"Cassie!" Rhys pulled his pants over his thighs and buttoned them.

"You dirty bastard—" Siobhan said through clenched teeth.

Cassie knew that tone. Her friend was in full-on savage mode. However, Cassie couldn't will her body or her brain to react. Rhys scrambled out of the car, shirtless, landing on the ground. Armed only with a designer handbag, Siobhan focussed on her assault, hitting him repeatedly while uttering obscenities Cassie had never heard before. Through the other door, Scarlett ushered out his accomplice, who was slipping a skimpy dress over her head. Amy O'Halleran. Jesus Christ. Two days before their wedding Rhys screwed the town slapper in the back of her car. She turned around and looked up at the night sky, willing the scene behind her to disappear.

"Cassie! Baby. It's—" Rhys called out.

"Don't you dare say it's not what it looks like you piece of shite!" Siobhan was relentless. The level of her anger should have been startling, but Cassie didn't try to stop her.

Time slowed as confusion gave way to humiliation. She broke into a cold sweat, clasping her hands together in an effort to stop the painful shards of despair thrumming through her veins.

She started walking toward the back door of Kennedy's, her family's pub, where she and the girls had spent the last few hours after their night of dancing at a local night club.

"Come on, honey, it didn't mean anything. I love you!" Rhys continued as she kept walking.

One foot in front of the other.

"Cassie, come on! We're getting married. That's for life! I was only saying goodbye to Amy."

She was vaguely aware of a groaning sound behind her and if she was a betting woman she'd say Siobhan had kicked Rhys square in the nuts. Her shaky hands fumbled with the door handle as a violent tremor overtook her body. As she staggered through the door of the pub the only words she remembered were his last. Obviously, it wasn't Rhy's first time taking Amy for a ride.

"What did you girls forget?" Nanna Kit held a tray of glasses in her hand. She stopped short. "Sweet merciful God, Cassandra, what's happened?"

Cassie stood in the doorway, clutching her handbag in front of her unable to speak.

"Cass, sweetie, let's get you inside." Siobhan's breathing was heavy and her face flushed. Probably from beating the piss out of Rhys. With one arm around her shoulders, Siobhan helped move Cassie through the doorway. "That mother fu—"

"What's going on?" Nanna Kit cut Siobhan off as she lay the tray on a counter and rushed to Cassie's side.

"He begged to come inside, but I told him to get lost before Colm gets his hands on him," Scarlett said as she closed the back door of the pub behind her, leaning against it.

"Get my hands on who?" Cassie's younger brother, laid his own tray of glasses on the counter near the dishwasher and stretched, stifling a yawn. "I thought you guys left. No more drinks. I'm going to bed." His eyes slid over Siobhan as he said the words.

The two had been engaged in this sport of long-standing flirtation for well over a decade and since neither of them could commit to an ice cream cone, this was the closest thing either of them had ever gotten to a long-term relationship.

Nanna Kit placed her hands on either side of Cassie's face, eyeing her granddaughter carefully. Cassie's eyes filled with tears and she flung herself into her grandmother's arms.

"Colm, bring in a bottle of Jameson's and four glasses," the woman commanded.

"What's going on?" he asked.

"Come on. I'll fill you in on the way." Siobhan grabbed his hand and the two slipped through a doorway into the pub.

"What did he do?" Nanna Kit whispered in her ear before pulling back to study Cassie.

"It's more like *who* did he do?" Cassie wiped at her eyes.

~

Cassie buckled her seat belt as her iPhone buzzed for the twentieth time today against her leg. She turned the ringer off hours ago, but a glance at the screen showed a string of texts and several voice mails waiting. She thought he'd have given up by now. After all, a month had passed. What was left to say? She held the button down and waited a few seconds, sliding the screen into the off position. When the phone went black she sighed. Maybe in the time it took to fly from Dublin to Las Vegas she could forget him.

Could you forget five years of your life in fourteen hours? It was worth a try.

"Hey Cass, you ok?" A hand reached out and patted hers. Cassie looked up into Siobhan's smiling face. Siobhan had been through nearly everything with her—kindergarten, high school, first break-ups, the death of her mother, and now her cheating fiancée.

She nodded. "I'm sorry Shi, I'm not sure this was such a good idea. Maybe we should have flown straight on to New York. I'm not going to be great company this weekend." As the words left her mouth, the plane surged ahead and her stomach dropped as it always did in that moment before the wheels gently lifted into the air. The landing gear whirred and thumped on its retreat into the plane's undercarriage.

Siobhan grinned. "Too late now, sister!" She squeezed her hand and Cassie's belly sunk a little. "How else should you drown your sorrows than by having a wild girls' weekend with your two besties?"

"Exactly," Scarlett said, leaning forward in her window seat, smiling at them both. "This weekend is exactly what you need, you'll see. Maybe you'll meet someone new." Scarlett held her boarding card over the lower half of her face, raising her eyebrows suggestively.

Tears stung her eyes and Cassie shook her head. "Not a chance. I'm off men for good."

"Forget about Rhys, he wasn't much of a man anyway," Siobhan said.

"Hey, I thought we weren't supposed to mention him or marriage on this trip," Scarlett said.

"You're right. We're not." Siobhan rubbed her hands

together. "This is going to be so great. Halloween in Las Vegas! I got us wicked costumes!"

Cassie raised an eyebrow at her friend, who bubbled with excitement. "Oh God. I am not dressing up as a French maid again, Shi."

Siobhan pointed her finger at Cassie. "Hey, you looked hot as all get out in that outfit Cass, but no, I've gone for something a little more refined this year. And I wasn't going to tell you this until we got there, but I have a huge surprise for you guys."

Siobhan's enthusiasm was infectious. She waved her arms, her big blue eyes brimming with excitement. Cassie hoped some of it rubbed off. Siobhan was a classic beauty: tall, athletic build, porcelain skin capped off by raven black hair. The black Irish, Cassie's mother used to call them.

A mischievous glint appeared in her eyes. "I snagged us an invite to Medicon's masquerade ball, only the hottest ticket in town tomorrow night!"

Cassie put her head in her hands. "No way, uh-uh." She shook her head. "Not happening."

Scarlett's feet tapped back and forth in front of her as she squealed with delight.

"Oh, come on, Cass, it'll be great," Siobhan said. "Dressing up on Halloween in the town that never sleeps? Wearing a mask and mingling with strangers and nobody knows who we are? It's so—"

Scarlett's eyes widened. "Sexy."

"Yes! That's the spirit, Scar! Seriously, can you think of anything hotter?" Siobhan nudged Cassie's shoulder with her own. "Come on, you need some harmless fun. You need to *be* fun again. It's been a long time." She smiled ruefully. "Rhys is a dick. The way I see it you got a get out of jail free card. Dodged a bullet. I know it hurts now, but that's the humiliation of the whole affair. The fact that everyone knows what happened. It'll pass. Trust me."

"How can you be so sure?" Cassie asked. "You've never gone through something like this."

"You're right." Siobhan nodded her head in agreement. "But we've all had a bad break up, or two, and you need to make your peace with yours and move on."

"I know that up here." Cassie pointed at her head. "But it's taking a little while longer to get the memo in here." She pressed her hand against her heart, stifling her grief.

"I know, but you'll realize soon enough that Rhys wasn't for you." Siobhan put her arm around Cassie and squeezed.

"He cheated on me so I know he wasn't the one for me. But it doesn't make it any easier. I had a whole life mapped out with that asshat."

"You need to meet someone who makes you feel excitement again. Exhilaration, longing, lust," Siobhan said. "Be honest. You never felt any of that with Rhys, did you?"

"Not in a long time." Cassie blinked to keep the threatening water works from spilling.

"Right. So, someone better is out there waiting for you. And you'll find him. Or he'll find you. But for now, think about a room-full of strangers and three of us dressed in black leather," Siobhan said.

"We're going as bikers?" Scarlett asked.

"Nope. Dominatrixes!"

"Oh, holy heart of Mary," Cassie muttered.

Scarlett whooped. "Shi's right. This is going to be amazing!"

"Of course it is! The three musketeers together for one last weekend in Vegas before Cassie starts her new life in

New York!" Siobhan smiled. "Have I told you how happy I am you found a job in the Big Apple?"

Cassie cast a side-glance at her. "You found it," she said. "And yes, you have mentioned that once or twice. I need to make a clean break from Kilkenny for a while. It's not forever, but it's for now." She peered into her friend's eyes. "Thank you."

"It was no hardship, believe me." Siobhan was a director with one of the largest headhunting firms in the US and had moved to New York City three years ago. She was after Cassie to move, but Rhys had zero interest in relocating to New York so the conversation had been a non-starter.

Cassie's public relations credentials were solid. The first day the job search started, Siobhan lined up three interviews for her by Skype within a few hours. All the interviews went well, but Crave's offer was the best. Being anonymous in New York was just what she needed. No pitying glances like the ones she received back in Kilkenny. In New York, there'd be no more humiliation and most importantly—no more Rhys.

"I cannot wait for this party!" Scarlett said as she and Siobhan coordinated details around make-up and props.

Cassie shuddered. She rested her head back on the seat and closed her eyes. She'd wallowed in self-pity for long enough now. Maybe this weekend was what she needed. After all she'd been through, it couldn't possibly hurt.

CHAPTER 2

THE ATRIUM OF THE BELLAGIO WAS NATURALLY COLOURFUL with its kaleidoscope of carpets, paintings, and floral arrangements but the large columns, coupled with outlandish Halloween decorations, gave the place a gothic vibe. There was some serious money here. Thanks to Scarlett's job as a manager at an international hotel chain, they were going to live like they had money to burn as well. She'd secured a suite for the weekend at minimal cost through some business contacts.

"Will you look at this place?" Siobhan's eyes darted over every surface as they made their way to the elevator and their suite on the thirty-second floor.

Scarlett slid the key into a slot. When it buzzed, the door opened to a spacious suite with a wall of windows and the stunning Las Vegas skyline as a backdrop. The lights of the strip twinkled in the late evening sky against the orange silhouette of the Spring Mountain Range.

"Sweet Jesus in the garden picking apples! This place is off the hook!" Siobhan dropped her bags in the middle of the floor and ran to the window first before skipping down the hallway. "And we each have our own room!" she yelled over her shoulder.

"Thanks for making this happen, Scarlett." Cassie squeezed her friend's arm with affection.

"Hey, it was nothing." Scarlett beamed in return.

The girls followed Siobhan inside one of the bedrooms as she collapsed onto a bed with her arms outstretched. She sat up and glanced to the corner of the room. "Is that a hot tub in the corner?" She raised her eyebrows suggestively.

Siobhan and Scarlett were giddy, but after a full day of traveling Cassie was exhausted. Every time she fell asleep on the plane thoughts of Rhys and Amy O'Halleran plagued her dreams. Damn him! The last thing she wanted to do was party. She'd rather put on her pyjamas and order room service, but she couldn't tell her friends that. This weekend was designed to pull her out of this funk and she owed it to them to be a team player.

"We still have a few hours before we need to dress for the ball. Why don't we head down and try our luck in the casino?"

Cassie raised an eyebrow. "I'm not much of a gambler, Shi."

"Oh, come on. It's only a bit of fun. You don't need to be good at it."

"I don't know how to play anything." *Come on Cassie—pull yourself up by the bootstraps.*

"You can put money in the slots," Scarlett said, "but that's boring."

"Let's find a roulette table," Siobhan said. "That's where the real fun is." She winked. "Come on."

Ok, you can do this. For them, she'd do anything. Cassie grabbed her purse and followed her friends down to the casino.

"Drinks?" A passing waitress asked as they stopped at a Blackjack table.

"Three, please!" Siobhan said. "Champagne. We're celebrating!"

"Oh yeah? Let me guess. One of y'all is gettin' married," the waitress said in a Texas drawl.

"Oh, it's better than that." Siobhan's laughter rang out as she grabbed Cassie by the shoulders. "We're not even giving her a chance to be a statistic!" A sly smile curled her lips.

"Amen to that, girlfriend." The waitress laughed as she walked away.

A chorus of congratulatory messages sounded at a nearby table, grabbing their attention.

"Look at that." Siobhan nodded toward the table. "See that guy there? He just placed a five-thousand-dollar bet."

Cassie's eyes widened and she held her breath as the cards turned up and a collective groan sounded around them. "What happened?"

"Ouch is what happened," Siobhan said. "The dealer's fourth card came up to make a twenty-one, which beat his inferior King-Queen hand."

It was gobbledygook to Cassie, but the man slammed his hand on the table and cursed as the dealer swept away all his chips for the house. The table was deflated and everyone grumbled and disbursed. The waitress returned a few minutes later with their champagne and accepted the bills Shi stuffed in her hand.

"To freedom!" Siobhan and Scarlett said at the same time, clinking Cassie's glass.

Cassie smiled despite the black hole in her heart and sipped her bubbly. They were great friends trying so hard to lift her spirits and she had to play along. She could get back to moping once settled in New York. Some commotion a couple of tables over caught their attention and Siobhan craned her neck to see what the fuss was about.

"What are they playing over there?' Cassie asked.

"Roulette. That's where we want to be, it's much better. Come on!" Siobhan grabbed Scarlett by the hand and headed in the direction of the table generating the excitement. Cassie downed the rest of her champagne and followed along.

Scarlett was brought up short and turned around, grabbing Cassie by the shoulders. "Merciful mother, will you look at them?"

"Mmm hmm," Siobhan said. "Men gambling in general is a turn on, but those three are something else."

Cassie eyed the crowd gathering around three well-dressed, sexy men, who commanded the roulette table. Two high-fived each other and were doing well by the satisfied looks on their faces. Cassie could see the appeal, they were easy to watch. As her eyes grazed over the third man, equally well-dressed but much more subdued, her heartbeat doubled and she let out a small gasp. His square jaw was accentuated with just enough stubble to be sexy and his dark hair was short in the back and a touch longer in the front. As Cassie assessed him from across the table, he looked up slowly and met her gaze. A jolt shot through her as his shockingly blue eyes looked directly at her. She blinked and looked away.

"Let's move closer," Siobhan said, coaxing Cassie and Scarlett forward.

They sidled their way through the crowd to get a front-row view of the show and quickly became part of the cheering section. Cassie didn't know what to cheer about since she wasn't sure what was happening in the game. It appeared that they placed chips on random numbers and placed a bet in the hopes that when the dice was rolled, one of the numbers came up. Surely, there had to be more skill involved. How could anyone waste money so frivolously? Judging by the cut of their clothes and the Rolex watch Mr. Blue Eyes wore, money probably wasn't much of an issue.

Siobhan shifted her way through the bodies until she reached the three men commanding the roulette show. Scarlett moved gracefully behind her, while Cassie bumped her way through the cluster of bodies and poking elbows.

"Hey," one of Mr. Blue Eyes' friends said to Siobhan. Cassie chuckled. That didn't take long. Siobhan was like sex on a stick. It never took more than ten minutes in a bar before men swarmed her. Cassie had once witnessed a brawl break out at a pub in Kilkenny between a football team who had all claimed to have eyed Siobhan first.

"Hey yourself. Looks like your lucky night?" Siobhan smiled at him and nodded at the table.

"I certainly hope so," he said, smiling. His eyes never left Siobhan's even as he motioned the waitress over to order drinks.

In no time, Scarlett was engaged in conversation with the other friend and Cassie was left standing next to the table without a wing man, which set her mind on a desperate search for a viable exit strategy. She hadn't dated in a long time. Not that she wanted to date, mind you, but everything that had happened with Rhys had shattered her self-confidence until there was little left. She didn't know how to look up at Mr. Blue Eyes and offer a simple greeting.

Come on Cassie, it's a simple hello.

She dragged her eyes from the casino carpet up over his black pants, noticing how they clung to his hips, and all the way to his fitted, charcoal dress shirt. Finally, she met those penetrating eyes and coughed. "Ahem…hi." She offered a tentative smile.

His eyes crinkled. "Hi," he said, a gentle smile crossed his lips, as if sensing her discomfort.

She shifted nervously and looked away. This was painful. The girls were hitting it off well with his companions. The cute blond touched Shi's arm and whispered something in her ear. Siobhan threw her head back and laughed her throaty laugh, a magnet like birdsong to the opposite sex. Cassie hoped the walls of their suite were sound-proof.

She sucked in a breath and turned back to him. "So, do you live here?" It came out a little higher pitched than she'd have liked.

A hint of a smile threatened to curl his lips. "Here in the casino? No. You?"

Her face grew hot. "No, of course not. I mean here in Las Vegas. I live in Ireland. Well, not—I'm moving." She smoothed her hands down the front of her skinny jeans. "I'm Cassie from Kilkenny." She stuck out her hand. Nice to meet you."

"The pleasure's all mine." His eyes twinkled with amusement as he took her hand. "I'm Dax." His full lips parted, revealing a perfect set of white teeth.

God, he was a work of art. The line of his jaw was square, drawn with precision, and a dimple appeared in his right cheek when he smiled. She bit her lip until it hurt. She'd just met this man and her heart fluttered in her chest like she was sixteen again. She shook her head, trying to shake the unwilling and unwanted feelings of attraction that had come over her. It made her anxious.

"Are you ok?" he asked.

"Of course. I'm fine. I just—I'm sorry, I need to take this." She fished in her purse for her iPhone, which was still switched off from the plane ride. She held up a finger and said, "Nice to meet you."

Cassie was desperate to get away. The roulette table was still crowded as another group of gamblers had picked up where the others had left off. Her friends were preoccupied with his friends and there was nowhere to turn. As if sensing her need to leave, Mr. Blue Eyes leaned against the roulette table with his body stretching back to allow some small space for her to slip by. The only way to get away from him was to get closer.

"Thanks," she said, wishing the universe would swallow her up whole. She summoned up a breath and moved closer, slipping through the small space between his broad chest and his friend's back.

That's when her nose was assaulted by the most delicious smell of leather and spice. Her heart raced. The friend talking up Scarlett backed into Cassie and she lost her balance, falling right against Mr. Blue Eyes' chest. His arms tightened around her, balancing her, but holding on a touch too long. She was so close her brain cluttered up with white noise like a transistor radio trying to find a signal. Her iPhone slipped from her hand and hit the floor and for a moment she didn't care. She couldn't move. More precisely she didn't want to move.

"Thought you had a call to take?" She was so close to him his breath fanned her nose. It was delicious. Cinnamon. She had to move before she melted into a mushy swooning puddle right there on the casino floor.

"What? Oh, yes right." She blinked a couple of times trying to look down between them to see where her phone had landed. His grasp on her never slackened. What was wrong with her? This guy was hot as balls and she couldn't get away fast enough. *No!* The sane part of her conscience called out to her. *He's a man. They're all alike. Run while you still can.*

He let her go and eased down to pick up her phone, handing it to her.

"Thanks." Her voice was breathy. Was it warm in here?

"Looks like you lost your call," he said with an arched brow.

She glanced down at the phone that hadn't actually rung and said, "Yeah, guess so. I should…" She pointed in the direction of the main hallway. "I'm going to go see who it was."

He smiled and her knees threatened to buckle. She turned in the direction of the piano bar and hurried inside, flopping into a big leather chair with a heavy sigh. What was that? She tried to collect her thoughts while taking advantage of the full view of the roulette table from her seat. Her friends were still engrossed in conversation with Mr. Blue Eyes' friends, but he was nowhere to be found.

"Can I get you something, miss?"

"Limoncello martini, please."

"Coming right up."

Cassie sighed and played with her phone. She was flustered as all hell. When the waiter laid the martini in front of her she downed it in two gulps and laid the glass back on the table before he'd turned around.

"Another one, miss?"

She nodded. "Keep them coming."

CHAPTER 3

"I look ridiculous." Cassie stared in the mirror. Siobhan's costume included fishnet stockings and a tight leather bodice that almost pushed her breasts to her chin. "Did you steal these boots from Lady Gaga's closet?"

"You look sexy as hell, Cass," Scarlett said, fastening her own earrings in place before handing a pair to Cassie.

Siobhan left no detail to chance. She'd scored black spider-web earrings. The spider sat in the middle of the web with a red jewel in the centre of its back.

"Do you know how envious I am of that fiery red hair and those amazing green eyes? And don't get me started on your body. Here, help me with this choker."

Cassie secured her friend's necklace as Siobhan bound into the room with three riding crops in her hand.

"Ta da! What's a hard-core dominatrix without a crop?" She snapped it in the air until it made a smacking sound. She let out a throaty laugh.

Standing in front of them with one hand on her hip that jutted out perfectly, Siobhan O'Mara looked every bit a dominatrix. She'd bring every man in the room to his knees and she knew it.

"There's no way in hell I'm hauling that around with me all night," Cassie said. "It's bad enough you've dressed me up like a cheap floozy from Fields Corner." She blotted the red Perfect Score Mac lipstick Siobhan insisted they all wear as part of the costume.

"Girl, you look like a high class call girl who blows American senators, not one of those dirty skanks from Fields Corner!"

Cassie couldn't help but laugh at Siobhan. The three of them lifted their wine glasses.

"Where is this party anyway?" Cassie said.

"I don't know. All I have is an address," Siobhan said.

"Is it here on the strip at one of the other hotels?" Scarlett asked.

Siobhan checked her phone. "No. It looks like a residential address. I have a number for a car service I called earlier. They'll be here for us around nine."

"A car service? Wow. That's a nice host," Scarlett said.

"That's a *rich* host," Siobhan said.

"I'm surprised you two gave up the new friends you made downstairs to go to this party? It looked like you were hitting it off." It was Cassie's last-ditch effort to get out of this ridiculous costume and check out the Bellagio's room service menu.

Siobhan smiled wickedly. "As it happens…they have their own invite to the Medicon masquerade ball."

Cassie stopped breathing. "All of them?"

"Why? Interested in one?" A wide grin spread across Siobhan's face.

"Don't be silly." Cassie hoped she didn't sound too defensive. She'd only spent a few minutes in his company, but his clothes were like a beautiful wrapping paper emphasizing the definition of his finely-toned body—the real prize underneath. This was not like her. She'd been about to get married a month ago and now she was comparing undressing some guy she met five minutes ago to unwrapping a gift. She shook her head to free the image from her mind.

"What's going through that head of yours, Cass?" Siobhan asked.

"Nothing." *Nothing she wanted to share.*

"I saw how you blushed when you were pressed tight against him." Siobhan came up behind her in the mirror and whispered in her ear.

Cassie's cheeks burned. Great. Now her face matched her lips. "It wasn't like that—" The ding of Siobhan's phone drowned her out. She blew out a breath. *Who was she kidding? It was exactly like that.*

"Car's here, ladies. Let's roll!"

Siobhan and Scarlett grabbed their black leather clutches and headed out of Cassie's bedroom where they had perfected their costumes. Cassie took one last look in the mirror and tried to pull the black leather bustier up a little higher, but it was useless. Mr. Blue Eyes would be in attendance. Heat rose to her face. She picked up her glass and swirled the last of her red wine before downing it. If it was a true masquerade ball, they'd all be wearing masks and no one knew who she was anyway.

~

After about thirty minutes in the back of a stretch limo they left the bright lights of the Las Vegas skyline behind them and entered the burbs; the high-end burbs. The only evidence of life was a glimpse of light that broke through the thick wall of trees lining the long driveways. There was some serious money here.

The car slowed and turned into a gate that opened automatically, winding its way through the tree-lined driveway toward a well-lit mansion decorated with intricate stone work. The elaborate fountains and light gave the place an old-world European feel. Dozens of costumed people lined a red carpet to enter. As her brain worked overtime to take in her surroundings, Cassie noticed the lack of pumpkins or nurses or silly costumes. This was serious. These people barely wore any clothes, and if they did, it was revealing and suggestive and they were all…stunning. It was like a prerequisite.

"Wow," Scarlett said. "This is amazing."

Siobhan whistled. "This is how I want to live."

The limo rolled to a stop and their door opened. "Ladies," a deep voice said and an outstretched hand assisted Siobhan, Scarlett and Cassie out of the luxurious car.

As Cassie stepped out and took in her surroundings she gasped. "Is this for real?"

"It is tonight." Siobhan slapped her ass. Cassie yelped and moved forward. "Come on ladies, I want in on this party!"

They took their place in the red-carpet line. When they reached the front, they were met by a man and two women. One woman gave them a plain black mask to fasten into place; the other gave them a token. Cassie turned it over in her hands. The number thirteen sparkled in the moonlight. She smirked. Unlucky thirteen sounded about right. The man stood behind a cloth-covered table with a glass bowl.

"Memorize the number on your token please," he said.

"What's this for?" Cassie held it up, examining it. Like everything else around her, it looked expensive.

A sly grin spread across his face. "First Medicon masquerade ball? Oh, you're in for a treat, honey. We have a reputation you know." The two women with him laughed.

"Sure do," one of them said. "Biggest balls in town." The three laughed again.

"Pop that token right in here, doll. In you go. You'll be scooped up in no time," he said.

Had he growled at her? Cassie scooted by him, dropping the token into the bowl with dozens of other pieces and followed her friends inside.

What the hell had Siobhan gotten them into?

~

If the mansion's exterior was impressive, its interior was like something directly out of a movie. The focal point of the atrium was a sprawling staircase, which lead in opposite directions from the landing. Floating above all of it was the largest sparkling, shimmery chandelier Cassie had ever laid eyes on. It looked like a hundred thousand diamonds glittered from the ceiling.

"What a pad," Scarlett said, turning her head slowly. She took out her phone and snapped a picture.

"Will you put that away!" Siobhan swatted her arm. "You're going to make us look like a couple of tinkers." She looked sideways at Cassie. "And what's with the puss on you? Will you at least try to have fun?"

Guilt flooded through Cassie. Siobhan had designed this weekend for her and she'd pulled out all the stops doing so.

"We're here. We're dressed to kill. And we're anonymous. That's the recipe for a great night, but you've got to want it. You can choose to have fun or you can go sit in the corner and let all this pass you by." She kissed Cassie on the cheek. "Hope you make the right choice."

She was a little uncomfortable about tonight, but Siobhan was right. It was time to give into it and let loose. She grabbed a glass of champagne from a passing waiter clad in nothing but a black thong and a white mask, and boy, was he ripped.

In fact, all the wait staff was barely dressed. They milled around the room, serving hors d'oeuvres and champagne. By the time she tore her eyes away, Scarlett and Siobhan had moved through an opening leading out of the massive house onto the grounds. Cassie stepped onto a sprawling stone patio, which surrounded a large pool with synchronized swimmers doing some funky Cirque de Soleil shit.

"Nice to see you again." The voice was low and husky.

Cassie stopped in her tracks, blood rushing to her head. She wore a mask and it was dark—well mostly dark. He could anyone recognize her? She turned around.

"H-hi?" It came out like a question. She waited a beat before looking up, but it was definitely Mr. Blue Eyes. In the flesh. She couldn't believe he was the first person she encountered in a crowd of at least two hundred scantily clad people. Though he was fully dressed in the same delicious outfit as earlier, he now donned a white mask. Not that it mattered. She'd know those eyes anywhere. She could get seriously addicted to them. Look away!

"How'd you know it was me?" she asked, averting her gaze to the pool and the wild show taking place there. Were they having sex? No way. Her Catholic upbringing made her question the plausibility of that thought because surely that could not be happening right here. In front of all these people?

He chuckled and his eyes stayed on her and not on the sex show behind her. "Oh, darlin' I'd know your—" his eyes raked her body and her face burned. "Red hair anywhere." His voice was husky. His eyes smouldering.

She laughed, a nervous chuckle. "I wasn't sure where you were going with that."

He placed an arm around her and leaned in, his lips inches from her neck. "I'd recognize you in a brown sack," he whispered. "And you'd still be the most gorgeous woman in the room."

She swallowed hard, catching the whiff of his cologne again. The same mix of spicy leather and outdoors. It was intoxicating.

He stepped back and locked eyes with her. "I have to be somewhere for a few minutes, but I'll be back. Will you wait here for me?" He pressed his lips lightly against her cheek. Dear God.

Would she be here? Yep. In a heaping pool of her own making, right here where she stood.

"Uh huh," she managed to choke out.

He flashed a brilliant smile and disappeared into the crowd.

A female voice sounded over a loudspeaker. "Ladies and gentlemen, would you please come together for the most exciting part of the evening. The moment you've all been waiting for. Ladies to the right of the pool. Gentleman to the left."

Cassie looked up at a woman clad in a skin-tight silver dress speaking from a balcony above the pool area. Women clustered around Cassie. Okay, she was on the right side at least. Good thing because she wasn't sure she could move if she tried. She glanced around, but Siobhan and Scarlett were nowhere to be seen.

"Ladies, please step forward when your number is called," the woman said. "Let the masquerade begin!"

Slow and sensual music sounded from some corner of this party and people moved and swayed almost as if they were under a spell. The man who had handed out the tokens outside the mansion when they first arrived appeared again with the glass bowl. He nodded to the first man in line, who stepped forward to choose a token.

"Twenty-two," the woman from the balcony said.

Cassie's eyes shot up. This was a sophisticated operation. The woman next to Cassie stepped forward and walked over to the man who had picked her token. He leaned in and kissed her briefly, whispered something in her ear and they moved off inside the doors of the mansion. The next number was called.

Cassie's heart thumped wildly in her chest. Do these people know each other? Surely, Siobhan did not have sex with strangers in mind when she said they were going to a masquerade ball! Cassie thought the worst that could happen tonight was that she'd get drunk and dance on a table, maybe stumble a time or two. There was no way she was staying for this.

She craned her neck, searching for her friends. The women around her buzzed with excitement. For a split second, she was furious with Siobhan.

"Number thirteen." Wait, what? Cassie froze. That was her number.

Her arm jerked. Nope. Not happening.

She needed to get out of here and fast. Before she had a chance to turn tail and run a man walked towards her. No fucking way! She was not doing this. She looked around trying to figure out an escape plan.

He stopped a few feet away and extended his hand, coaxing her forward. Her breath hitched. It was Mr. Blue Eyes. Cassie's mind raced, but she moved toward him. Wait. What? When she was near enough, he took her hand and pulled her in close. Whispering in her ear he said, "Hey, looks like it's my lucky night."

The hair on the nape of her neck lifted. Cassie was speechless as he placed a chaste kiss on her lips. When he pulled away his smile was wickedly sexy and Mother of God—those eyes. She melted right there on the spot.

Have fun Siobhan had said.

Could she do this?

~

He crossed the room and sat on the bed, watching her. She leaned against the door, eyes pinned shut, hands behind her back. She raised one leg and fixed her high-cut leather heel to the door. She was fastened to it like a magnet, knowing that if she moved she might fly into this man's arms and that thought terrified her to no end.

"I don't bite." His voice oozed sex. She opened one eye. He was sitting on the end of a king size bed on the other side of the room, elbows on his knees, leaning slightly forward, watching her. He could be an axe murderer for all she knew. A handsome one, though.

"Don't you?" she managed to croak out.

He threw his head back and laughed. "I could, I suppose, if that's what you're into. But you don't look like that kind of girl to me."

"Ha." She almost snorted. "You don't know the half of it."

"I bet I do." His eyes raked her over. "Let me guess.

Your friends dragged you here under false pretences and you can't wait to get out that door."

"You read minds too?"

He chuckled again. "I've seen that look before."

"You do this a lot?"

He frowned. "No, but I saw you walk in tonight and I took it as a sign." He stood up slowly and closed the distance between them not once taking his eyes off her. He took off his mask and tossed it on a chair in the corner of the room. Those eyes. They were seriously blue like cornsilk. Like, almost not real.

"Did you randomly pick my number?"

He stopped and placed his hands on either side of her head against the door. "Can't fight fate, right?"

She couldn't think. The spicy leather smell of him filled her head and those eyes looked at her like she was the only person in the world. She took a deep breath. Did she care? "Are all these people pairing off to have sex?" she asked. The instant she said it she regretted it. He'd think she was a prude.

He smiled. "Is that so terrible?"

"I'm from Ireland. It sounds like the work of the devil."

"You're funny." He smiled and lifted off her mask. "And beautiful." His thumb took an extra second to slide across her cheek before he tossed the mask to the side. He placed his hand against her heart."Is that for me?" he whispered.

She nodded slowly. Her heart pounded in her chest. His lips grazed her neck while his hands slid up her body before getting lost in her hair.

"I don't think I can do this." She was breathless as he brushed kisses along her jawline and across her cheek. His hands slid down her back coming to rest on her leather-covered ass.

"I'd never make you do anything that made you uncomfortable." His lips were a breath away from hers. "You can leave whenever you want." His lips found hers again and this time he kissed her. Like really kissed her. She groaned into his lips and her belly fluttered as he smiled briefly against her mouth. It was shockingly intimate. How could she feel such a connection to this man?

In between kisses he said, "Do you want to leave?" He didn't wait for her response. His lips devoured her. This kiss was more urgent than the last, with his tongue darting out to make her open wider. Cassie gasped, her hands suddenly coming to life sliding up his thighs and resting on his chest. His rock-hard chest.

As her body's grip on the door loosened, his arms slipped around her waist and he turned them around, leading her toward the bed. He picked her up like she was a feather and rested her head on the pillow. He guided them down gently and settled next to her, never once breaking their kiss.

It wasn't just any kiss. It was an all-consuming, toe-curling, never-forget-as-long-as-you-live kiss. Cassie had been with Rhys for five years and not once had they shared a kiss as passionate as this. A nervous excitement filled her to the core. As he shifted closer, his hardness pressed against her leg. Behind her, his hands moved to unlace her corset. As he pulled the strings loose, her breasts spilled out of the leather bodice and he broke the kiss long enough to catch one of her nipples between his teeth and suck hard.

Cassie writhed beneath him, her hands tugging his shirt out of his pants. She may have said she couldn't do this a few minutes ago, but her actions contradicted her mind. She touched his slender hips and when the shirt was free, she ran her hands over the washboard abs hidden underneath. She groaned again. This couldn't be real.

"Does that mean you're staying?" He found her mouth again. His tongue darted in and out, tasting her, exciting her, making her light-headed. Lifting himself until he straddled her, he hooked his fingers in the fabric of the leather bodice by her thighs and tugged. He slid the whole piece off in a matter of seconds and her breath hitched as the cool air hit her nipples. In an instant, he covered her with his chest, leaning down to kiss her neck and behind her ear.

"You're gorgeous," he whispered.

A kaleidoscope of colours appeared behind her closed eyelids. This only happened in movies and romance novels. Not to Cassie Kennedy. Home-grown girl next door, Catholic-guilt-to-the-core, Cassie Kennedy. Every nerve ending in her body was on high alert. And it felt good.

She fumbled with the buttons of his shirt, but when she realized his lips were no longer on hers, she brought her fingers to her own swollen lips. She opened her eyes. He was still straddling her, but had leaned back to slip his shirt from his broad shoulders and toss it to the floor. She instinctively sat up, sliding her hands over his torso and she laughed.

"You're laughing at me." He raised an eyebrow.

"No, I'm not," she said, still laughing.

"I'm pretty sure I know what laughter sounds like." He crawled up next to her, settling on his side and he reached out to caress her arm. "Should I be offended?" He kissed the base of neck.

She shook her head. "No. God, no. I truly wasn't laughing at you," she said. "You're perfect."

"Am I?" He grinned.

"I was laughing at the absurdity of this situation. You don't understand. I don't meet strange men at parties and do *this*." She waved her hand in his direction. "I mean—I can't do this." Tears clouded her vision. "God, I was supposed to be married for a whole month already and instead I'm here in Las Vegas letting a stranger peel my clothes off."

Dax sat up, pulling the pillow from underneath him and placed it behind his head. Suddenly conscious of the fact that she lay there in nothing but stockings held up with garters, all part of Siobhan's grand costume idea, she sat up and folded her arms over her chest, too embarrassed to meet his eyes.

"Hey," he said, lifting her chin up to meet his gaze. His eyes still smouldered, but she could tell by his gentle demeanour he'd never force himself on her. A look of understanding crossed his face and he moved away long enough to reach for his shirt on the floor. He helped her arms into it and wrapped it around her.

Once she was safely covered she looked at him again. "I'm sorry. The fates weren't kind to you tonight."

"I'll be the judge of that." He pulled her close and she rested easily against his chest. "Now, why don't you tell me why you didn't get married a month ago?"

She leaned back and looked up into his kind face. "I'm sure you don't want to hear about that."

"I'm not going to lie to you, I'd rather be kissing that mouth of yours, but that's not what you need right now."

Cassie leaned back against this stranger's chest and told him all about Rhys's affair. She broke down a time or two, but he urged her to keep going, his arms tightening around her at her most vulnerable points. Later, when she couldn't talk anymore he kissed her senseless until they fell asleep tangled in each other's arms. Not only did she drift to sleep in Dax's arms, but she did so without another thought for Rhys and Amy. She did so with a peacefulness she'd not enjoyed since her world came crashing down.

~

She woke with a start, a heavy arm draped across her stomach. The room was dark, but a sliver of light from the full moon outside cast enough of a glow in the room that she appraised the man beside her. She memorized every detail, knowing she'd never lay eyes on him again. His strong shoulders and smooth chest. She cast a rueful glance at his abs. "Bye-bye perfection," she whispered. My God he was absolutely beautiful. And his mouth. Cassie covered her swollen lips and smiled. She couldn't wake him, he looked too peaceful.

Cassie slid out from underneath his arm and quietly slipped out of bed. Searching in the darkness for her clothes was a challenge, but she pulled all the articles together and threw them back on. She bet she didn't look nearly as put together as when she'd entered the house, but at this point, she didn't care. The girls probably thought she was sulking in a corner somewhere.

She tied the bodice as best she could by herself and stole one last look at the bed. He was like a statue of muscle and hard body lying there in nothing but his pants and a tangle of white sheets. She was about to step out this door looking every bit like she was doing the walk of shame and no one would believe she didn't have sex with this man. But what she'd shared with Dax was much more precious. He listened to her. He sympathized with her. He kissed her. Oh, did he kiss her. But he expected nothing in return.

The Catholic school girl inside was still embarrassed that she'd entertained the thought of pairing off with him at all, but there was no point in going there. She'd never see him again, so she wouldn't die of embarrassment. The thought of not seeing him again saddened her. He was so kind and gentle and so the opposite of Rhys. It was nice to be wanted by Dax. It gave her back some of her self-esteem. She'd get through this and come out the other side. She put her hand on the door and looked back one more time at the perfect specimen of a man she was leaving in bed.

"Goodbye Mr. Blue Eyes and thank you."

Thanks to him, come Monday she'd start that new job in New York with a spring in her step.

CHAPTER 4

"RISE AND SHINE LOVER BOY." A SERIES OF KNOCKS JARRED Dax from the longest uninterrupted sleep he'd had in years. He opened his eyes and blinked at the bright light filling the room. He rolled over, a lazy smile tugging at the corner of his lips. Something akin to panic shot through his veins as his hand spread over the cold sheet beside him. The warm body he'd cradled half the night was nothing but a memory. Another short burst of knocks followed and he sat up, scrubbing the side of his face with his hand.

"Yeah, I'm up." The door cracked and his buddy Zander peeked his head through the opening.

"Where's your little fire engine?" He nodded at the empty spot on the bed next to Dax.

Dax shrugged. "Gone, I guess."

"Smart chick."

"What's that supposed to mean?" Dax swung his legs over the side of the bed and scanned the room for the shirt he'd wrapped around Cassie last night before kissing her to sleep. He spied it neatly folded on the cushion of a wing-back chair. He crossed the room in two strides and retrieved it, looking discreetly for a note, a card, anything that told him something about the girl consuming his head this morning.

"She left before you had to break it to her gently. You know, she saved you the trouble of the old—I don't do relationships, sweetheart—don't call me because I definitely won't call you speech." Zander studied Dax. "Real hammer to the pride being the leave-ee instead of the leaver, huh?" Zander laughed.

Dax did not. Zander's description of him was a bit unnerving. Was he that much of a jackass to women? He hadn't cared for a woman in a long time, that much was true. Caring leads to love. Love leads to heartbreak—world-obliterating heartbreak. He didn't have that in him again. There was too much at stake now.

"Breakfast downstairs in ten. The caterer is setting up now."

"Yeah, okay, be right down."

Dax shrugged his shirt on. The fabric brushed his face and stopped him in his tracks. He breathed deep—sweet, feminine and all Cassie. He knew nothing about her or how to find her. He cursed himself for sleeping so sound. When was the last time that happened? He frowned. She mustn't have wanted him to know she was leaving. The thought filled him with disappointment.

Zander was right. He'd been the love 'em and leave 'em type for a long time now. Anything else was too risky. Up until now he hadn't given much thought to how it may have affected the women he'd been with. It's not like he left a relationship discussion on the table. There were a few women he'd seen more than once, but they understood the stakes. He controlled the where and when and, above all else, they understood there were no strings attached. He paced the room and the source of his distress finally hit him—Cassie held the balance of power here. She left without giving him any options. Well, it wasn't any fun being on the other side, was it?

He finished buttoning the shirt and reached for his watch on the nightstand when a thought struck him. He'd met Cassie at the Bellagio. Odds are she returned there after she left him. He glanced at his watch. It was only seven-thirty. With any luck, she was staying another day. He had to get back to the hotel, but first he'd have to endure breakfast and the ribbing his buddies were going to lay on him for believing he'd finally hooked up at one of these parties.

There was no way he could explain what had happened in this room a few hours ago, but it wasn't a simple hookup. No, it was much more than that. Ordinarily, the thought would scare him, but instead he counted the minutes until he could lay eyes on the utterly captivating redhead that had taken up residence in his mind. *Time to wipe that shit-eating grin off your face, Dax—you haven't found her. Yet.*

~

It was a little after nine-thirty when he finally reached the Bellagio and headed straight for the front desk.

"Can I help you, sir?" A pretty hotel receptionist smiled.

"Hi. I'm a guest here, Room 2760." He flashed his room key. "I'm looking for a woman by the name of Cassie." He shot her a dazzling smile. "I also know that's not a lot to go on. Can you look in your system to see if you get a hit with just a first name?"

"I can, but it's highly unlikely. It's also against our policy to give out her room number."

He leaned in closer. "But, if by some stretch of fate you do find a Cassie, you could call up and tell her Dax would like to see her in the lobby. That wouldn't be breaking any rules, right?" He'd like to see her in his room, alone, but he'd settle for the lobby.

"Well, let's see if I can find her first. After that, we'll see what else I can do." She smiled and clicked a few buttons on her computer.

He scanned the lobby while he waited, analyzing any female that had as much as a red highlight in her hair. He had terrible luck. While he stood back on to the lobby, she'd probably walk right out the front doors like in some cheesy romance movie.

"I'm sorry, sir. I'm not able to see anything with Cassie on it."

Dax thought back to when he first met her at the roulette table. "She was with two friends. Hard to miss. Three beautiful Irish women, a red head, a blonde, and a brunette." He realized his description sounded a bit like the beginning of a bad joke or an episode of Charlie's Angels. He also may have sounded more than a little desperate. "Do any of them ring a bell?"

She shook her head. "No. Sir, I see a lot of people in the run of a day." She gave him a half smile. "I'm sorry I couldn't be of more help."

"That's okay. Thanks." He tapped his hotel card on the granite counter and turned around to head to the elevator bank. A man behind the concierge's desk waved him over.

"Excuse me, sir. I couldn't help but overhear your conversation. You're looking for the three Irish women?" he asked.

"Well, one of them, yes, but I'd settle for all three right now," Dax said.

"I got them a car to McCarran about forty-five minutes ago."

"Fuck." He couldn't contain his frustration. "I'm guessing you have no idea where they were headed?"

"No," he said. "But I'll tell you what." He beckoned Dax closer and grinned. "The driver's a friend of mine. I'll call him and find out which terminal he dropped them at."

"Thanks, man."

"Let me guess." He picked up the phone and paused before dialing. "The red head?"

"Yeah." Dax cocked his head and raised a brow.

"Figures. That chick is smoking," the concierge said as he waited for his friend to answer.

You have no idea. Dax tapped his foot and leaned against the concierge desk, waiting for any scrap of information that might lead him to her.

"Hey, Tony, those three Irish girls you brought to McCarran. Which terminal you drop them at?" The concierge covered the bottom of the phone with one hand. "Terminal one. American Airlines."

"Thanks." Dax took out his wallet and grabbed a twenty-dollar bill. "I guess he doesn't know where they were headed, does he?"

"Thanks Tone," the concierge said, hanging up the phone. He pointed his finger at Dax, "I could lose my job for this, so you better not be a serial killer."

Dax couldn't help but laugh. "Nah, I'm not a serial killer. Just a regular guy who hasn't met a woman like that in a long time."

"In that case, there may have been a discussion about New York City."

A slow grin spread across Dax's face. "Thanks, man." He put the twenty back in his wallet and exchanged it for a fifty. He placed it in the concierge's hand and grasped it in appreciation.

With a wide grin, he crossed the lobby to an elevator and stepped inside, leaning back against the wall. His search field had gone from the whole of the United States to one state. One city—his city. The fact that New York happened to have eight and a half million people in it was a minor detail.

~

It took the taxi a little more than a half an hour to drive from LaGuardia to Cassie's brand new apartment on West 56th. She opened her phone looking at the photos of the place and smiled. When Siobhan had texted her pictures of the apartment, she'd known by the square footage alone it was way out of her price range. Of course, Siobhan continued torturing her with pictures showing the view of the city from inside. There wasn't a chance in hell she could afford it. But leave it to Siobhan to finagle a deal. Since her friend had left Ireland, she'd somehow found a lucky horseshoe and had it permanently wedged up her behind.

As it turns out the apartment belonged to a friend of a friend's father, whose daughter and boyfriend had lived there. After a sudden break-up, the boyfriend moved out and the girl fled New York to travel the world and find herself. She was in Italy now and had apparently found herself, and a handsome man, fifteen years her senior, who owned a lucrative winery. According to Siobhan, the girl had no immediate plans to return. Her father just wanted it rented to someone responsible and reliable. Siobhan had assured him the only woman holier than Cassie Kennedy was Mother Theresa. She signed the lease, agreeing to pay a little over half what the apartment was worth and the rest was history.

Scarlett had flown back from Vegas to spend a few days in New York with them before she returned to Dublin. They had taken a separate cab to Shi's place and Cassie had promised to meet up with them later for dinner. She was lucky to have friends like them. If she'd ever questioned the level of their devotion to her, she'd never again after this month. They had her back at every turn. Held her while she cried. Cleaned out her stuff from the flat and did everything they could to make Rhys's life a living hell in the process.

Not living in Ireland was going to be different. It's all Cassie had ever known and a small part of her felt guilty for leaving her family behind. But they were a big crew and eventually they all left the nest for a while to explore the world or find themselves. The road always lead back to Kilkenny, to her large and colourful family and to Kennedy's Pub.

She leaned against the window as the evening set in and the taxi traveled over the Robert F. Kennedy Bridge taking her into Manhattan and to her new home. Never in her wildest dreams did she think she'd be in New York City. She loved Ireland and thought nothing could match its beauty with endless stretches of green fields, surrounding much of the small city of Kilkenny. But New York's skyline was a majestic backdrop of vibrant lights and colour and the shimmer sparked an excitement in her. She was ready for something new.

Her phone dinged again and she hesitated, hoping it wasn't another lame attempt by Rhys to contact her. But it was only Nanna Kit, who had already texted her several times. In a previous text, she'd told Cassie to stay with Shi for a few weeks till she got that dirty sleveen—Rhys—out of her system and come home. Cassie opened the messages app and laughed.

NK: Treasure, remember to keep a container of mace in your pocket.

CK: What for?

NK: Your Uncle Mac says the place is totally uncivilized. You'll want to be gettin' home before some wild lad with a funny accent ravages you, steals all your money and leaves you for the rats in a backstreet alley.

Cassie leaned her head back against the seat and laughed. Nanna Kit's words were never designed to frighten. They were her way of telling Cassie she could always come home. Not that she needed to be told that. She had a wonderful family, but this move to New York was about new beginnings and independence and she was excited about the promise of a new life here. But she also couldn't get someone else out of her mind. Mr. Blue Eyes. Dax. She'd certainly left Ireland and her old life with a bang. Her eyes wandered back up to the line that read, before some lad ravages you. Cassie closed her eyes and thought about her late-night encounter.

The girls had teased her the whole flight to New York. She spent most of it in her own little world, dreaming about Dax's hands roaming her body. She'd left Ireland heart-broken. It was like mourning a death. The death of a relationship she'd built everything around. She planned a life with Rhys and mapped out her whole future with him and in an instant, he'd stripped it away with one careless, callous action. Rhys's infidelity had left her vulnerable.

While thoughts of the evening still brought heat to her face, she decided she wasn't going to let embarrassment ruin her memories of their time together. Dax gave her back some confidence last night. He wanted her. Caught her eye over a roulette table, of all things, and manipulated a game to land her in his bed. There was no way he picked her token by chance. The thought was intoxicating. It was purely physical. What was so bad about that? Whenever that Catholic guilt seeped back in again and her cheeks warmed thinking about their activities, well, she put it out of her mind because she'd never see him again. A saddening thought.

He'd never know he was responsible for her good mood, the dazed smile she'd been wearing, and her serious case of day-dreaming. Thoughts of Dax's hands on her and the way he held her tight consumed her again until she heard a polite cough.

"Hey lady, I ain't got all day ya know." When she looked up the cabbie was staring at her in the rear-view mirror with a look that said he'd been stopped a while now and the meter was still ticking.

"I'm so sorry," she said. "Off in my own little world." She opened her purse. "What do I owe you?"

"Fifty-five." She thrust three twenties at him before exiting the yellow taxi and looking up at the monstrous high-rise. Her new home. He retrieved her suitcases from the boot of the cab and laid them next to her.

"Thanks."

"Mm," he grunted, sliding back in the cab and speeding away.

A doorman appeared. "Miss Kennedy?" he asked.

"Yes."

"Come right in." He took both her suitcases and ushered her inside. "I'm Charlie." Once they were inside he parked her suitcase near the front desk and turned around, sticking out his hand. "Doorman here for nearly twenty-five years."

"Lovely to meet you, Charlie." She guessed he was early sixties. He had a pleasant face, a full head of silver hair and kind eyes.

He walked around the desk and retrieved an envelope. "Mr. Lannigan said you'd be arriving this evening and that I was to give you these." He opened the envelope and placed a set of keys in her hand. "He's sorry he couldn't meet you himself. His granddaughter is getting christened today. But he'll be by tomorrow evening to run through everything with you and give you the grand tour of the building."

"Okay, thanks."

He took her suitcases and led her inside an elevator, pressing buttons on the key pad. When the elevator doors opened to the twenty-first floor, he wheeled her suitcases down the hall to a corner apartment.

"Thank you so much for your help."

"No problem, Miss Kennedy. Do you need anything else?"

"No, I think I've got it from here."

"You have a long evening ahead of you, I suspect." He chuckled.

"I doubt I'll accomplish much tonight. I'm knackered. Still adjusting to the time difference, I'm afraid."

"All right, I'll leave you to it."

"Have a good evening, Charlie."

"You too, Miss Kennedy, and welcome home." He tipped his hat before stepping inside the elevator doors.

She turned the key and the apartment door swung open. Her belongings had arrived in New York about a week ago and the superintendent, a fellow countryman, had overseen its placement in the unit. She groaned at all the boxes, some of her excitement fading. She looked around at the black leather furniture and the expensive paintings on the wall. At least the place came fully furnished. She stepped inside and closed the door behind her.

Home.

Well, Cassie, you're not in Kilkenny now are ya old girl.

CHAPTER 5

Cassie stepped onto the New York City sidewalk and breathed in the crisp November air. New York at seven-thirty in the morning was a sight to behold. The streets were jammed with traffic as taxicabs and cars competed for the same limited space. People spilled onto sidewalks from subway stops in all directions, hurrying toward their destinations. Some sipped coffee and others talked on phones, their animated voices and colourful accents echoing through the concrete jungle.

The sound, combined with the smells from the street vendors, catering to their loyal customers, all came together like one big orchestra reminding Cassie that the Big Apple was about as far away from Kilkenny as there was. It was everything she'd ever imagined life in New York City would be like. Now she had to figure out how Cassie Kennedy fit into this big city life and all it had to offer.

The Franklin Building was about a twenty-minute walk from her apartment and there was no better way to get to know the neighbourhood than to walk it on her first day. However, she was seriously rethinking the stiletto heels she donned. If she was going to do this walk every day she was going to have to sacrifice fashion for comfort. As she fell into the stop and start rhythm of pedestrian traffic, she was bewildered by the sheer volume of people on the sidewalk, crossing the street at one time. She'd woken up several times last night, a little restless and excited. Each time she drifted to the window that overlooked the street below. It didn't seem to matter the hour, pedestrian traffic was steady, but this was one of its peaks right now, the rush hour, marking the start of the daily grind.

As she reached the Franklin Building, she rifled through the emails on her phone until she found the one from the HR director, allowing her to pass through security. As she exited through the metal detector and into the wide-open atrium, she heard someone call her name.

"Cassandra Kennedy?"

Cassie turned to face a striking woman, tall, slender, with coal black hair and eyes to match, in her early thirties walking toward her.

"Yes."

"Right on time. I like that." She held out her hand. "Hi, I'm Gina Lombardi, the HR director."

"Hello Gina." Cassie shook the woman's hand. "It's nice to meet you. Thank you so much for the opportunity."

"Hey, we're happy to have you," Gina said as she led Cassie into the elevator and pushed the button. Cassie grinned and looked down at the floor. Undoubtedly, Siobhan had exaggerated Cassie's sudden demand in the United States. The doors almost closed and opened again at least five times before the tiny box filled with people. Cassie found herself pushed back against the wall with a woman's handbag thrust in her chest. The one thing she'd learned in an hour was that New Yorkers had no real regard for personal space.

Gina looked over at her. "Great resume by the way. Love the social media campaign you created for that not-for-profit arts group in Ireland. Very creative. I think you're going to love your team."

"Thanks," Cassie said as the elevator surged upward. After several stops to let the crowd out, the doors opened into a spacious foyer with a tall, black, front desk and two perfectly sculpted young women seated at the helm, wearing headsets. Cassie glanced around at the open-concept design of the office. The few walls were painted white and the rest of the offices were separated by glass. In the centre was a big boardroom. People hurried about the long table, distributing materials that looked like the precursor to a big meeting.

"Wow, it's um—" Cassie took in the colourful artwork, the glass partitioned offices and the perfectly dressed men and women who inhabited them. She was speechless. The space was sleek and chic and like nothing she'd ever seen.

"You like it?"

"What's not to like?" This was the big leagues and she was about to step into the batter's box.

Gina laughed. "Oh, honey, we're getting to that. There's the late hours, the insane deadlines and the competing interests, but I think I'll let you enjoy the honeymoon period first before I rain on your parade."

Cassie chuckled. Several tall, good-looking men passed by. All of them said good morning and at least two of them shot Cassie a backward glance with a smile.

"Good morning Miss Lombardi. You're looking particularly lovely today," the last one said.

"Bobby, honey, your flattery doesn't work on me. And besides, we both know you're just wondering who the new girl is. Most mornings you can barely afford me a grunt, let alone a good morning. Keep on moving. Nothing to see here."

Bobby clutched his heart and scrunched up his face. "Ah, you wound me Miss Gina."

"Yeah, I bet. Watch that one Cassie, he's a real ladies man." Gina laughed.

"Ouch! Gina, baby, if I turn around will you take that knife outta my back? It's going to be hard to sit at my desk all day with it stuck in there like that." He pretended to be trying to remove something from between his shoulder blades.

"I'm serious, Bobby, move along. Don't scare poor Cassandra off on her first day." Gina swatted the man on the shoulder as he continued down the corridor. He looked back at Cassie and mouthed call me, placing his thumb and pinky finger along his face as if to intimate holding a phone.

"Looks like you have a bit of fun around here."

"We try not to take ourselves too seriously. Sometimes we succeed." Cassie followed Gina down a hallway to the left.

"Wow. All the women look like they stepped out of Cosmo and all the men looked like they just stepped out of GQ," Cassie said.

"If you think that handsome string of hotshots is something, wait till you see our CEO," said Gina.

"Yeah?"

"Oh yeah." Gina swooned, pretending to fan herself. "But he's off limits," she said, a warning tone in her voice.

"No worries here." Cassie shook her head. "Believe me, I'm not interested in men." Gina raised her eyebrows. "Right now. I mean, I'm not interested—" Cassie coughed and Gina laughed.

"Listen—women, men, whatever floats your boat. It's

2018, right?" Gina put her hands in the air. "No judgement here."

Cassie laughed. "No, no, it's not like that, though I'm glad to see you're liberal-minded. I meant I'm swearing off men for a while." She was sworn off one for damned well sure.

Rhys had sent hundreds of texts and countless voice mails. She hadn't returned one. The last message she listened to last night made her so angry, she contemplated tossing her mobile phone in a dumpster. He'd said her silence was unfair and demanded she see him so he could get some closure and that she owed him that much. She owed him? Two things were evident: he had no idea she wasn't in Kilkenny and if the affair with Amy wasn't proof enough of Rhy's selfishness, that message sure was. What an asshole. Siobhan was right—she'd dodged a bullet.

"If he were on offer I'd be the first in a long line, but he is off the market in a big way." Gina stopped abruptly and turned to look at Cassie. "Okay, you ready?" Cassie nodded and Gina opened a door, pulling her inside a spacious corner office framed by windows.

Cassie clutched her handbag and moved in a circle, taking in her new surroundings. She walked over to the windowed wall overlooking West 59th Street and 5th Avenue.

"This, my dear lass, is your space," Gina said in an attempted Irish accent, complete with a little dance.

Cassie guessed it was supposed to resemble Michael Flatley's *Riverdance* and she burst out laughing, covering her mouth.

"All right that was terrible. Sorry. I'll stick to my Brooklyn accent. I've got that one down cold." Gina grinned.

The full effect of the office hit her and Cassie stopped

laughing. "Wow! This is brilliant. I love it!" Like everything else she'd seen this morning, it was modern and impressive. The office was spacious and designed with minimalism. A black credenza, adorned with straight brushed nickel hardware, lined the wall to the right. She wandered over and ran her hand along the frosted glass oval desk in front of the credenza. She leaned against the glass and faced Gina, taking in the two, cream-coloured and very comfortable-looking leather chairs facing her new desk. To the left of the room a meeting table with six chairs sat clean and empty with a vase of fresh flowers in the centre. "I don't even know what to say."

"Great! I hope it inspires you," Gina said. "I suspect you'll be breaking out your creative side in a few minutes. Apparently, there's a big campaign coming up, the details of which are being rolled out this morning. In fact, I would be introducing you to your team right now, but Mr. CEO himself has summoned us all to the main boardroom for nine. As Crave's new Director of Marketing and Communications, you'll need to be there."

"Of course." Cassie nodded.

"Good. So, on your desk you'll find your security pass. You'll need that to get on the floor and into the building. You'll also find an iPhone, or your virtual leash as I like to call it, courtesy of Crave." Gina leaned in and winked. "Once you turn that on you belong to us day and night. Consider your social life over."

"No problem," Cassie said, meaning it. The sad reality was her life *was* work. There was nothing waiting for her in her apartment except boxes.

"I'm kidding. Well mostly. Okay, I'll give you a few minutes to get acquainted with your space. There's a bunch of forms on your desk, payroll, benefits, the usual. Have a look and we can go through it later. IT already set up your computer earlier this morning. Temporary passwords are posted on your screen for initial log in." She looked at the phone in her hand. "Meet me in the boardroom in fifteen minutes and I'll introduce you to the team."

Cassie laid her purse in the comfortable chair behind the desk and turned to stare out at the view. It was truly incredible. Over a month ago she'd been cheated on. Her wedding cancelled. Now she was standing on the thirtieth floor of a New York high rise about to embark on an amazing new job and life, leaving all her heartache behind. She was a new woman since waking up in Vegas on Sunday morning. She had a new lease on life. So why the sudden pang of sadness? And why did it have more to do with the man she left in a bed in Las Vegas than her fiancé of five years in Kilkenny?

Cassie found her way to the boardroom fifteen minutes later with her phones in hand and a black book for taking notes. She had even taken a moment to group text her nearest and dearest with pictures of her new office and a quick note to let them know she was settling in. She placed her book on the table while her new colleagues engaged in friendly banter about kids, partners, weekends and plans to get together soon. Without doubt, they'd worked together for some time.

"Hey, Cassandra." Gina waved her over. Cassie smiled and joined a group of at least fifteen people. "Everyone, this is Cassandra Kennedy all the way from Ireland. She's our new Director of Marketing and Communications and boss to the six of you." Gina pointed at a group of four women and two men standing together. "These two hipsters locked in deep conversation—" She pointed back and forth between the pair. "Are your photographer and graphic artist. Best of the best."

"Aw, thanks Gina. Hey, Cassandra. Welcome to Crave. I'm Josh, the photographer." The taller of the two stepped forward and reached out his hand. Not only was he dressed like he'd just stepped out of a trendy New York magazine shoot aimed at millennials, but he also looked like he was fresh out of high school. Peering at the young faces on her team made Cassie suddenly conscious that her thirtieth birthday was about to steam roll her. These were youngsters!

"You can call me Cassie," she said, taking his hand. "Only my father calls me Cassandra, and that's before he's getting ready to tear a strip off me."

"I'm Luke." The other one said. "And we're more than pretty artists." He shot a brilliant smile at her. He was dramatic, impeccably dressed, and unquestionably gay.

The others laughed and introduced themselves one by one. In addition to Luke and Josh there was Cara—the copywriter, Serena—the event planner, Portia—the public relations manager, and Cristal, yes, like the champagne—the social media guru.

"All right people, take your seats. Carter's on the floor." A woman stepped into the room, ending the social gab as everyone grabbed a chair around the boardroom table. She passed a stack of folders to the first person seated, who proceeded to take one and hand them down.

Cassie sat next to Gina, who gave her a reassuring smile. It had only been an hour, but already Cassie sensed Crave was a good fit. The people were friendly and the work promised to be interesting. She'd had a lot of trepidation at dropping her old life and leaving everything she'd ever known in Kilkenny for a new life in New York City, but she could do this. Her thoughts slipped back to the man she'd met Saturday night and she picked up her pen, letting it wander around the blank page unprompted by conscious thought.

"Good morning." The voice came from behind. It was smooth and sophisticated, friendly, but firm—yet oddly familiar. "Let's jump right in since I only have forty-five minutes between meetings. I'll keep my presentation to twenty minutes and you get twenty-five for a round table. Sound good?"

Goosebumps prickled Cassie's skin as a delicious scent accosted her senses. Her ears and nose were on high alert and the rest of her body followed suit. She couldn't shake images of sexy, blue-eyed Dax and her body's reaction to thinking about him was startling. Time to tune it all out. Hit the ignore button. Concentrate. She turned to a clean white, empty page—symbolic of her new life and all the promise it held.

"I understand our new Marketing and Communications director has arrived," the talking suit said, rounding the table to take his place at the helm.

A nervousness pulsated through her and she fought the impossible thoughts flooding her mind. *It couldn't be.* Her mind raced. One thing was clear—her overactive imagination was trying to sabotage her first day.

"Yes, sir," Gina said. "We've got Cassandra Kennedy on deck this morning." She shot a wide smile in Cassie's direction. When her eyes connected with Cassie's the smile faded and Gina raised an eyebrow.

Cassie willed her eyes to the head of the table.

Three.

Two.

One.

"Welcome Miss—" the suit stopped cold.

Cassie winced as she broke from Gina's questioning

stare and leaned forward, dragging her eyes to the man easily commanding his post at the head of the boardroom table. A brilliant smile highlighted his handsome face, one of those rare smiles that reached his eyes.

His blue eyes.

Sweet baby Jesus.

It *was* him.

CHAPTER 6

IT WAS HER.

He'd seen the flaming hair the minute he entered the boardroom. He'd noticed more redheads in the last twenty-four hours than he had in a lifetime. His heart thumped so loud it echoed in the hallway. He had written it off as ridiculously hopeful, but here she was. In the flesh. He fought the urge to clear the room and have her all to himself, but that would raise a few eyebrows. Her eyes flickered when they met his and he'd stopped talking. In fact, he'd stopped breathing.

He hadn't been able to shake the memories of her and their night together in Las Vegas. Knowing she was probably high in the sky, he'd still roamed the gates of terminal one at McCarran International yesterday, studying every redhead seated in the waiting area, hoping one of them was her. It wasn't like him to take part in Zander's outlandish hook-up parties. He'd never done so in all the years they'd been friends, but Halloween night when she walked in, he realized he'd have done anything to spend time with her. He'd been enchanted with her since their encounter at the roulette table. That gorgeous mane of red hair, her milky white skin and green eyes weren't easily forgotten. Her shyness was more endearing and he liked the way her cheeks reddened from his longing looks. Coupled with her accent and smoky voice—he was gone.

When she'd showed up at the party he took it as a sign. The look on her face told him she was more than a little intimidated by what was happening. All the better for him. Armed with only her first name and physical description, he'd gone to Cheyenne, Zander's PA, and insisted she retrieve Cassie's token. He couldn't risk someone else doing God knows what to her. He knew the moment he met her she wasn't the one-night stand type.

The guys had razzed him hard at breakfast. They'd seen him go into the house with Cassie and while he raised his hands in protest, denying that anything had happened between them, they didn't believe one word of it. The funny thing was they didn't have sex, but something happened between them. Since Marley his encounters with women had been random hookups with zero expectations —purely physical and never with the promise of anything deeper. Just how he needed it. But the night he shared with Cassie in Las Vegas was the most intimate he'd been with a woman since his life turned upside down. If her soft sighs as she returned his kisses was any indication, she must have felt the same way.

His eyes darted to Gina Lombardi's, whose eyebrows were raised so high they'd soon be lost in her hair. Her head turned back and forth between him and Cassie. Her eyes held questions, which she'd never be bold enough to ask him, but Cassie was fair game. He'd love to be a fly on the wall for that conversation. What would Cassie say about him? About them? He suspected she wasn't the kiss and tell type. He couldn't stand here staring at her all morning. Hell, he was supposed to be running the meeting. *But she was right in front of him.* Only seconds had passed, but it felt like hours, days. He tried to maintain composure, but his thoughts returned to forty-eight hours ago.

They had kissed and touched until they fell asleep wrapped in each other's arms. He thought he'd get a phone number or an email from her in the morning, but she'd left without a word and it had rattled him. Last night he had even scoped out a private investigator to find her in a city of millions. He stared down the table again, locking eyes with her. She broke the connection quickly, casting her eyes to her notebook, her face reddening. His cock twitched to life. He wanted to smile, hell he wanted to sing, but here in front of the staff he couldn't do any of those things. He needed to get this meeting over with and talk to her. The look on her face became strained, almost uncomfortable and he realized she couldn't have known who he was, he'd never given her a last name. She'd been hired at Crave before the trip to Las Vegas. It was fate. And fate was sitting in his boardroom. Reality hit him like a sledgehammer. How could she possibly fit into his life?

The answer was simple.

She couldn't.

~

Roulette wasn't the only thing the man was good at. He had a killer poker face too. If Cassie had blinked, she'd have missed the flicker of recognition in his eyes. He nodded politely in her direction, eyes pinned on her for a few seconds. Long enough for Gina to kick her under the table. She'd have to deal with that later, but he launched right into the presentation he came prepared to give without casting another glance in her direction.

Only two nights ago he'd seen her mostly naked. He'd kissed her mouth, her breasts. Her face warmed as the memories of his sensual mouth on her sensitive body parts flooded through her. Cassie crossed her legs under the table. Except they weren't only memories now because the man responsible for them was right here standing in front of her and by the looks of things he was her new boss. How could we have not discussed work? *Because your mouth was busy doing other things.*

My God, she'd ruined what could have been the best night of her life by crying on her new boss's shoulder about her love life! At a sex party. Make no wonder he couldn't look at her now. The prude, whose staunch morals kept her from having fun her whole life. The burden was like carrying a talisman designed to be a killjoy, destroying any chance of fun in this life.

Cassie had held out for the longest time with Rhys. Finally believing he was the great love of her life, she'd finally given herself to him and where had that gotten her? He'd betrayed her trust and ruined their life together. She'd been going to spend the rest of her life with him. Dax had been a gift to take her away from all the heartache and self-doubt and she'd wasted it. She'd wasted that mouth of his by talking and pouring her heart out, instead of doing the wicked things she'd secretly wanted to do.

She continued to hit the home button on her phone to check the time. Forty-five minutes, that's what he said. She only had to get through forty-five minutes of this torture. So much for waking up in Vegas yesterday like a new woman. Today, she felt worse than when she'd found Rhys and Amy O'Halleran in the back of her car.

~

When the meeting ended, Cassie leapt from the table and shot out of the boardroom as fast as she'd ever moved. Gina called her name, but she kept going. She was lost in the glass maze for at least ten minutes before she found her way back to her office and plopped in her chair, turning to the wall of windows, facing the city below. She stared at the bustling street.

Maybe Siobhan could find her another marketing job. She found this one easily enough. Surely, there were plenty more in the city. One of her phones dinged. She picked up her personal phone. It was probably Nanna Kit after getting the pictures of Cassie's new office. The phone dinged again and she realized it wasn't her personal phone at all. It was her work phone.

Unknown ID: Can we talk?

CK: Who is this?

Unknown ID: Who do you think it is?

She swallowed hard.

CK: I haven't the slightest. I've met a lot of people today.

Unknown ID: You met me first.

Heat pooled between her legs.

CK: I thought you had another meeting?

Unknown ID: I canceled it.

CK: Why?

Unknown ID: It isn't obvious? Where are you?

CK: In my office.

Unknown ID: And where is that?

CK: Great question. I have no idea. Shouldn't you know that?

She continued staring at the screen though she knew she'd hear his sexy voice and smell his tantalizing scent within minutes.

"Cassie." She spun around slowly in the chair until she

faced him. He leaned against the doorway, hands in the pocket of a steel grey suit that fit him so perfectly she could almost make out the sculpted lines of his stomach. No, that was her memory taking over, reminding her she'd already touched every sculpted line of his stomach.

"Mr. Carter."

He narrowed his eyes, challenging her conventional address.

Cassie, the minute this man kissed your breasts the formality ship sailed.

"Dax."

His eyes raked her body. They slid from her face down the silk ivory-coloured blouse, tucked into a black Haider Ackerman pencil skirt, all the way to her nude Christian Louboutin pumps. Siobhan had loaned her the shirt and skirt for her first day. Cassie didn't have a budget for high-end clothes like that. The Lous were hers, purchased after she hawked her engagement ring. A gift to herself.

"You left," he said.

"I know." She bit her bottom lip.

"I never thought I'd see you again."

"Sorry about that." She ran her hands down the front of her skirt.

"What are you sorry for? Leaving without saying goodbye or spending the night with me?"

"Yes. No." She shook her head. "I'm…" she trailed off, trying to find the right words. "I'm a bit embarrassed by the circumstances under which we met. It was a big mistake. Siobhan made me dress up in that stupid costume." She winced and placed a hand over her forehead as if the thought caused her pain. "She talked about a masquerade ball, but none of us knew it was *that* kind of ball. I mean, honestly, I've never been to any ball before, but I'd definitely never been to one like that!" She placed both her hands on her face, almost cradling it so her head wouldn't explode.

He stepped inside her office. As he did so, Gina appeared in the hallway. Her eyes widened when she saw him there and if she'd intended to stop, she thought better of it. Cassie's eyes flickered to Gina and Dax turned in time to see her scurrying around the corner. He closed her office door and hit a button along the wall Cassie hadn't noticed before. The glass walls frosted over instantly, giving them complete privacy.

"It was all a mistake?" He scrubbed his jaw.

She stared at his jawline, remembering she'd kissed it a few nights ago. She'd never noticed how tall he was before. Probably because she'd spent all her time with him lying down. He was lean, at least six two and had broad shoulders. Powerful. Her mind flashed back to her last image of him lying shirtless, tangled in a mess of sheets, looking perfectly fuckable. Again, the heat crept to her face, a recurring theme around this man.

"Dax. I didn't mean—"

"Because it sure didn't feel like a mistake when I was kissing you."

"I—" He came a few steps closer, placed both hands on either side of the empty desk and leaned over her. His dizzying scent hit her just like she knew it would.

"If you want a new life here in New York with a clean slate and no strings attached, Cassie from Kilkenny, that's up to you and you'll get no bother from me. But don't pretend you didn't feel something in Las Vegas. Don't pretend there's no connection between us."

Cassie held her breath as his blue eyes pinned her in place. If anyone else stepped inside they'd be electrocuted by the live flow of electricity between them.

"Who said I was pretending?" She stood and leaned

across the desk to meet his stance. His eyes smoldered with heat. He opened his mouth, but the sharp ring of his phone silenced him. He straightened and held up his index finger to indicate he needed a moment.

"Hello," he said into the phone. He stepped back from the desk and walked across the room.

Cassie fell back in her seat and blew out a breath. Tension screamed in every muscle. She looked at the frosted glass windows. That was an impressive feature and she appreciated it right now, but how was she going to explain this? Gina had seen Dax step into her office. The last thing she needed was for Gina or anyone else to think she was getting any preferential treatment from the boss. It was her first day of work. Talk about a career-ender.

Dax's voice rose and she glanced over to where he was standing. With his back to her, he still exuded confidence, power and pure sex. A throbbing between her legs sent a rush of heat to her face. If this kept up, she was going to have to stash extra panties in her purse. He abruptly dismissed his call and walked back to her desk.

"I have to go."

"Okay."

"I can't believe you're here." A softness flickered in his eyes.

"I know, but—" She licked her lips. "You're my boss."

"You're a director here. You don't answer to me."

"A technicality."

"A reality." She was drawn to the heat of his stare. "I have to go, but this isn't over," he said.

"What is this?"

"I don't know yet, but I'm sure as hell going to find out."

He left her office without a glance back, which was just as well since he may have seen her jaw drop. Cassie sat in her chair and stared at the spot he'd been standing in for an eternity. Her better judgment told her to resist Dax if she wanted to get off on the right foot here at Crave and earn the respect of her colleagues, but it was clear he wasn't going to make that easy.

Cassie tried to clear her mind, but she didn't recall any details of the briefing she'd attended twenty minutes ago. She hoped her staff were as good as Gina said they were.

CHAPTER 7

"GET THE FUCK OUT," SIOBHAN SAID AS SHE SHOVED A piece of moo shu pork in her mouth.

Scarlett and Siobhan sat on the floor of Cassie's new apartment eating Chinese take-away while Cassie filled them in on her first day, including the awkward, yet panty-dripping encounter with Dax.

"It's fate," Scarlett said, refilling their plastic cups with wine. "He was handsome, I remember."

"And, your boss." Siobhan pointed a chopstick in Cassie's direction.

"Believe me, I know that." Cassie groaned. "It can't work. Plus, I'm fresh out of a relationship, which had a dramatic end. Everything in me screams that this is a bad idea. Until I'm looking in those piercing blue eyes." Cassie winced. "And I melt."

"Ugh, enough with this fate bullshit. You know what your problem is ladies?" Siobhan asked between mouthfuls. "You form attachments too easily. Sometimes good sex is just that. It doesn't have to be anything else."

"Yeah, about that—" Cassie started.

"I mean, you're enamoured with this guy." Siobhan cut her off, digging deep in her take out box. "But that's only because he's the first guy you slept with since that arsewad, Rhys—the devil incarnate. Dax's sidekick, Zander, equally yummy, gave me his number too, doesn't mean I'm going to call him."

"Forgive us if we don't take relationship advice from you, Shi. You never call anyone. All part of your bad girl act." Scarlett snorted.

"It's not an act," Siobhan's tone was sharp.

"You forget we know you." Scarlett screwed up her face at Siobhan, who threw a napkin at her in return.

"I never slept with him," Cassie said. She might as well have hauled out a sword and challenged them to a duel—it had the same effect.

Siobhan's diatribe came to an abrupt halt.

"What?" asked Scarlett.

Cassie shook her head. "I mean I slept with him. Next to him. But there was no sex." She had their full attention now. "Oh, believe me, I wanted to. But I couldn't. Instead, I cried my heart out. I told him how Rhys had cheated on me, how humiliating it was, how I cancelled the wedding, the moving, all of it." Cassie sipped her wine as the girls stared silently. "And he listened," she continued. "To every word. And we—well, we may have fooled around a bit." She coughed. "But we fell asleep in each other's arms. That's it. End of story." She searched her friends' wide eyes.

Siobhan's jaw dropped and, as any good friend would, Scarlett closed it to prevent the Singapore noodles from spilling out. After a minute of silence Siobhan took a big gulp of her wine.

"Well, that certainly changes the landscape," she said.

"How so?" Cassie asked, swirling the wine around in her cup.

"If Dax Carter barged into your office today, wondering why you left him in a bed in Las Vegas without a forwarding address, after you cock-blocked him at a sex party, the man's got it bad." She raised her plastic cup to Cassie. "Well done yourself."

The next few days passed in a blur and without any further contact from Dax. Cassie waffled from anxious to disappointed, but had finally fallen into a productive work pattern without looking over her shoulder, waiting and hoping, but knowing the longer she went without seeing him the faster she could get him out of her system.

As she expected, Gina had asked a dozen questions about Dax's presence in her office that day, but she brushed it off by explaining that he stopped by to welcome her, but also had asked some general questions about Ireland since he was considering vacationing there. Gina studied her with a "do I look like I fell off the turnip truck yesterday" look at first, but Cassie moved on to work topics and never gave her a chance to revisit the issue.

Cassie's team was worth their high praise and she was well up to speed on all their accounts after a few meetings. They were creative and savvy and she was looking forward to digging into the files with them. A knock on the door broke her thoughts and she looked up, heartbeat quickening with anticipation. She held her breath.

"Hey, do you have a minute, Cassie?"

"Yeah, sure Serena. Come on in." *And breathe out. The roller coaster ride continues.*

Serena was a perky blond, mid-twenties, but already

Cassie could see she was responsible and conscientious. She was a copywriter, but was destined to run her own projects in future. Cassie didn't want to lose her yet, though, since she was fast becoming her right hand.

"It occurred to me that you probably don't know anything about the dinner tomorrow night at the Museum of Natural History," Serena said.

Cassie cocked her head to the side. "You'd be right about that."

"It's their annual fundraising gala. They're a client of Crave's, obviously."

"Why obviously?" Cassie raised an eyebrow.

"You don't know much about New York's elite yet do you?" Serena smiled.

Cassie shook her head. "Haven't had much cause to before now."

"Okay, well here's a small crash course. Crave is a company under the Franklin Roberts consortium. Franklin's wife, Helen, is the chair of the museum's board. Which of course means she raises all their money."

"Ah, okay," Cassie said.

"Then there's Zander Roberts—one of the heirs to the Roberts throne. He's also the CEO's best friend." She laughed, moving her hands together like she was solving a Rubik's Cube. "They're all kind of interconnected, you know?"

Cassie's ears piqued at the mention of Dax's friend she met in Las Vegas.

"Anyway, Crave does a lot of work for the museum and they always graciously give us invites to the gala."

"I wouldn't call an invite to a fundraiser gracious, Serena, I'd call it smart." Cassie laughed.

"Well, since our table is paid for by Franklin Roberts and everyone else pays five thousand dollars a plate, it's a pretty gracious invite," Serena said, grinning at Cassie's arching brow.

"Let me guess, black tie?"

"Yup. I RSVP'd for the team weeks ago and included a place for you, though we didn't know it would be *you* specifically." Serena pointed at Cassie.

"I can't go to this, Serena, I don't have anything fancy to wear." Also, it was highly likely Dax would be there—yet another reason to avoid going. Visions of him in a tuxedo flooded her mind, not that she could admit that to one of her staff.

"Oh, don't worry about that. My friend manages a consignment shop in Soho. She gets fancy dresses all the time and lets me and Cara and a few other girls here borrow stuff when we go to these types of events. I'm sure she'll hook you up too, if you want." Serena smiled. "I can put in a good word for you."

All her staff was going so her absence would be conspicuous. She'd think of it like a team-building exercise in fancy clothes with champagne and socialites. It could be fun. If Dax was there it promised to be interesting.

"That'd be great, thanks," Cassie said.

The next evening, Cassie stepped in front of the full-length mirror in her bedroom and admired the dress Serena and her friend Jade had helped choose the day before—an emerald green, cap-sleeve sheath dress with a V-neck that accentuated her generous D-cup. When she had stepped out of the dressing room yesterday evening, the girls had catcalled, declaring the dress was made for her.

The rich brocade fabric was a magical green, making it hard to know where to look first. The cut of the dress accentuated her curves and highlighted the flame in her hair, which she wore down tonight, in loose waves around her face. Jade had also lent her a vintage, pear-shaped, diamond halo necklace and earrings to match. When Jade had tallied the price tag for fun, Cassie nearly had a stroke. Jade laughed and said there was nothing to worry about unless she ruined the dress or lost the jewelry, which only half-calmed Cassie's nerves.

She promised Serena she'd meet her and the rest of the team outside the museum at seven so she stuffed her keys into a black clutch and stepped inside the elevator. As the doors opened in the lobby, Charlie stood behind the desk and did a double take. "Well, aren't you a sight for sore eyes."

She smiled. "Thanks, Charlie. It's a work dinner."

"Ain't no one gettin' any work done at your table tonight, ma'am," he said. "You stay here while I flag you a taxi. You'll cause a ten-car pile-up, waiting out on the street like that."

"Oh, you're a smooth talker." Cassie laughed.

He tipped his hat as he stepped outside and returned a minute later. "All right Miss Kennedy." He held the door open. "Let's get you on your way."

It was less than a fifteen-minute taxi ride down Central Park West to the museum and traffic was steady, but not too slow. Not for the first time tonight did she wonder if Dax would be there. It didn't matter if he was or not. She was going with her team and it was a good opportunity to get to know them all outside the office. When the taxi stopped in the queue of cars dropping people at the museum, she tipped the driver and stepped out, eyeing Serena and the others near the entrance.

"Hey everyone," she said upon approach. "You all look great!" Luke and Josh looked smart in their tuxedos. Rentals, of course. Men had it so easy. Serena, Cara and Portia had all taken Jade up on her offer to borrow evening wear from the shop. Cristal was the only exception; she wore a designer dress all right, but Cassie couldn't say who it was. A lifetime in Kilkenny meant she didn't frequent galas or have much cause to attend black tie affairs. She knew the difference between a salad fork and a fish fork though, courtesy of her sister, who managed a fancy house for an English family in Kilkenny.

"You look amazing, Cassie," Luke said, leaning forward to kiss her on both cheeks. There was a chorus of agreement from the others.

"Thanks, guys. It's all down to Serena. The girl's got taste." Cassie shot her a wide smile and squeezed her hand. "Shall we get inside?"

"Not without a group shot on the red carpet," Josh said. "Come on. Follow me." The six of them fanned around Cassie while the photographer took several shots. Josh offered Cassie his arm. "Madame, may I escort you inside?"

"It would be my pleasure." She linked her arm with his.

They stepped inside the museum's atrium and were encouraged to pose for photos in front of a white façade half-wall, sporting the museum's logo. It was an impressive set-up and there were a few reporters and gossip rag writers covering the evening. Cassie insisted on another group shot of the whole team. Behind the wall, the main area of the museum had been transformed into an elegant ballroom. Millions of tiny white lights dotted the ceiling, giving the impression of a soft star-lit sky. Round tables set with elegant gold-rimmed dinner plates and crystal stemware sat on one side of the room like a Martha Stewart set design, while couples danced to a swing band, performing on a raised stage on the opposite side of the room.

The whole scene was surreal and Cassie surmised what Julia Roberts must have felt like in *Pretty Woman*. People clustered throughout the room as unseen wait staff, baring hors d'oeuvres and champagne, slipped between them. She accepted a glass from a passing tray and sipped. She'd never attended anything this elegant before. It was exciting. She was in New York City at a gala dinner, and dressed to kill. If only Rhys could see her now—he'd choke. She smiled.

Giddiness washed over her as she took another sip and scanned the room again. Her heart stopped. There *he* was next to the bar, drink in hand, looking every bit as dapper as she imagined in a tuxedo tailor made to fit his splendid body. His blue eyes twinkled and he laughed easily at one of the men telling an animated story. She recognized his friends from Las Vegas, but this time there were females in the mix, including a striking, well-put together brunette, who was every bit Dax's equal in the looks department. She touched his arm in a possessive way and he leaned in, whispered something in her ear and she rubbed his arm with familiar affection.

Unable to watch anymore, Cassie wheeled around, needing to look elsewhere as shards of hurt and disappointment shot through her. Come on. Did she expect him not to have a date at a high society function? No—but she had a serious case of wishful thinking. In that moment, she pictured herself next to him, those blue eyes gazing at her, and sharing in the laughter with his group of friends. The reality was the more she observed Dax in his natural environment the more she realized how far out of her league he was. They may have shared a steamy kiss or two that could have led to more if she had let it, but that's all it was. Pure. Unadulterated. Lust.

"Hey, red, you clean up real nice." Cassie blinked out

of her pity party trance and into Bobby's smiling face. He leaned in and kissed her cheek, lingering a little longer than necessary, but Cassie got the impression he was harmless enough.

"Hi Bobby, nice to see you," she said, happy for the distraction.

"You better save me a dance," he said as he pulled away and reached for a glass of champagne from a passing tray.

"Of course," she said, smiling.

"Cassie, would you excuse me? I see someone I've been trying to get a meeting with for months, but I'll be back." He called out to some guy named Mike and moved off.

Guests were taking their seats and she scanned the room for her colleagues. There were so many people here she'd lost sight of them in the crowd. She remembered the seating chart was on an easel near the room's entry point and she turned in that direction when a hand fell on her lower back. The touch was so new yet already familiar and it stopped her cold.

The mouth next to her ear whispered, "I said I'd know you in a brown paper sack. And this is definitely not a brown paper sack." His hot breath skimmed her neck, lighting every nerve ending in her body.

She shivered.

His hand found hers and he spun her around to face him. "Hi."

"Hi." She barely had breath enough to utter the word.

"You look amazing." His eyes never left hers, telling her he'd already done a full appraisal.

"You don't look so bad in a penguin suit either." She smiled and surprised herself by tugging on his bow tie. She pulled her hands away quickly.

His mouth curled into a delicious smile. She couldn't take her eyes off his lips.

"Why didn't you tell me you were coming here tonight?" he asked. She met his gaze and gasped at the heat in his eyes.

"I only found out about it yesterday. My whole team is here." She glanced around the room. "Though, I don't know where they are now." Looking back at him she said, "And besides, I didn't know we were exchanging schedules." She cocked her head to the side.

"Dax, darling, we're sitting now." The brunette hanging off his arm earlier appeared at his side.

"You go on, I'll be right there." He dismissed the woman without his eyes ever leaving Cassie's. "Cassie—"

"I think that's your cue." Cassie lowered her gaze.

She was determined he wouldn't see how disappointed she was. She shouldn't be anything. She hardly knew him and he certainly owed her nothing.

He wrapped an arm around her waist, pulling her close. "You're leaving with me tonight." He tilted her chin up to look at him again and she gasped at the yearning in his eyes.

"Your date might have something to say about that."

"It's not what it looks like."

"It never is." She leaned up and kissed his cheek. "Good night, Dax." She stepped back and walked away, the heat of his stare sliding over her the whole way.

She held her breath as she made her grand exit, unable to breathe. Everything about him consumed her and she couldn't think straight when he looked at her with those eyes. That penetrating lust-filled stare told her he could do wonderful things to her if given the chance. She heard her name called from across the room and her eyes scanned the tables. Luke and Josh waved their arms and she was never so grateful to have someone waiting for her.

Cassie didn't know what Dax's game was, but he was clearly less available here than he was in Las Vegas. A few days ago, she'd thanked him for giving her some confidence back. He'd removed some of the blackness shrouding her heart. Today, she cursed him for making her think he might have been her silver lining. She didn't know how these New Yorkers lived, but Cassie had no intention of becoming anyone's Amy O'Halleran.

CHAPTER 8

"Are you going to sit there like an asshole all night?" Zander slapped Dax's back as he laid a glass of scotch in front of him. "Drink this, maybe it'll mellow you out a bit."

Dax had sat, white-knuckled, at the Roberts' table all evening while practically every man, young and old, took Cassie for a spin on the dance floor. Hands down, she was the most beautiful woman in the room and Dax wanted to whisk her out of here and get her alone. Images of her on the bed in Vegas and his hands roaming her luscious curves flooded his mind. All these men saw was eye candy—a gorgeous woman in a smoking hot dress and heels. They could hardly be blamed for admiring the package, but Dax knew what lay underneath.

Since finding out she was Crave's newest employee on Monday, Dax had done a little digging. He'd studied her resume top to bottom. She was an impressive woman. She'd spanned a ten-year career in marketing communications, with a lot of her work focussed in the arts and not-for-profit sector. She wasn't all about big corporate and name brand accounts, which told him she was a deep thinker and cultured. She was smart, funny, and far more interesting than the rest of the dull socialites in the room. Lucky for him, he happened to also know what was underneath that green dress she sported tonight, which left little to the imagination. He'd spent all week telling himself Cassie Kennedy wasn't a luxury he could afford, but when he saw her tonight he knew he'd failed miserably.

"It's been a competition to see who's been boring a bigger hole in the back of her head all night—you or my sister," Zander said, leaning close enough so only Dax could hear him.

"Don't be ridiculous."

"Listen man, women are strange creatures. The claws come out when they sense a shark circling."

"Yeah, well, we both know your sister, of all people, has no right to get her back up," Dax said.

Zander shrugged and sipped his scotch.

He scanned the dance floor again and his eyes landed on Senator Hauxley's hand, a little too low on Cassie's back for Dax's liking. He downed the scotch Zander had placed in front of him and stood.

"Go get her big guy. Don't worry. I'll handle Vanessa." A wide grin overtook Zander's face. "You got it bad, Carter. Looks good on you."

Dax had never been drawn to a woman in his life like was to Cassie. He teetered on the edge of control. He had no allusions to the fact that people were watching him and when he walked out of here with Cassie on his arm, he'd trigger a series of events he could no longer control. There would be consequences. He'd handle those, but he couldn't let her walk out of here tonight with some jackass like Bobby Antonelli, who'd been sniffing around her all night like a tiger on the prowl.

"Senator, may I?" Dax asked, halting the dancing couple.

"Dax Carter, good to see you, young man." The two shook hands. "Your company did some great work on my campaign last year."

"Thank you," Dax said. "It was our pleasure. Congratulations, again, sir."

The senator gestured towards Cassie. "By all means. Thank you for the dance, Miss Kennedy." The older man gave Cassie a quick kiss on the cheek. He grabbed Dax's arm on his departure and pulled him in. "Don't tell my wife, but that redhead is the most beautiful creature I've ever seen."

Dax's smile tightened. Didn't he know it. He nodded at the senator and turned back to Cassie. She stood there, watching him. He reached out his hand and she slowly, deliberately placed her hand in his. He pulled her close, her lush breasts pressing against his chest. As the first few notes of Etta James's *At Last* sounded through the ballroom, Dax tightened his hold around her small waist. There wasn't enough space to fit a sheet of paper between them.

"I—"

"I want you," he said unapologetically as her face flushed.

"Dax." Cassie looked down.

"Don't look away." He tilted her chin to meet his eyes.

"I can't help it. You make me nervous," she said. The corners of his eyes crinkled, making her smile too.

"Do you know how hard it's been watching you dance with all these men tonight?"

"What can I say? I'm a good dancer," she joked.

"You're a better kisser."

She stopped breathing under his heated gaze. "Dax."

"Let's get out of here," he said.

"What about your date?"

"Don't worry about Vanessa. Zander will get her home."

"That's charming." She raised an eyebrow. "I don't know what kind of arrangement you've got with your girlfriend." He opened his mouth, but she raised a finger to stop him. "And it's none of my business. But I'm not going to be part of hurting her feelings. After everything I've been though, you of all people should know that." Her voice cracked.

It finally hit him how terrible the situation seemed.

"I told you it's not what it looks like." He brushed his thumb along her bottom lip. "Do you trust me?"

"I haven't had a lot of luck with trusting people lately," she said. "And besides, trust is earned."

"I'd never do anything to hurt you, Cassie. I promise I'll explain everything in the car."

She stared at him and for a few seconds. "You're sure of yourself."

"I'm sure I need to get out of here. With you. Right now." For a minute, he worried she wouldn't agree.

"I need to get my purse and say good night to everyone."

He nodded. "I'll meet you out front in five minutes." He pulled her against his chest and her thigh fell up against the hardness of his erection. She looked up in surprise. "That's what you do to me, Cassie Kennedy." His teeth brazenly grazed her ear lobe. "And I'm going to have you tonight. In that dress."

Her breath hitched as she gazed into his piercing blue eyes.

Dax helped Cassie into the back of a limousine before sliding in next to her.

"Good evening, Mr. Carter. Where to, sir?" The driver's voice filled the space through an intercom.

"Good evening, Carl. Great question. Where are we headed, Miss Kennedy?" He smiled, hoping she wouldn't ask why he wasn't taking her to his place.

"Oh, yes, hello," she said, looking at the ceiling of the car as if Carl was up there.

Dax chuckled. He leaned closer, taking her hand in his. He kissed each finger before he placed her hand on the console between them where the intercom button was located. As he moved back into his space his lips brushed her cheek. Her face heated under his touch.

"Oh," she said. "Right. I've never actually driven in one of these before." She coughed and pressed the button. "One thirty, West 56th Street, Carl. Please."

Just one more reason he was so captivated by her. She wasn't like the socialites who tried desperately to catch his eye. She stole a sideways glance at him and he covered her hand with his, a smile tugging at the corner of his lips.

Cassie looked out the window at the glittery New York lights passing by. The heady scent of him affected her ability to think so if she was going to ask for an explanation she had to do it now.

"Tell me about your date." She turned in the seat to face him.

He kissed her hand again. "Vanessa Roberts. Zander's sister. And we're just friends."

"Does she know that?"

"She does."

"I've got a lot of friends, but they don't hang off my arm all night and insist I take my seat with them, right this minute." Cassie tapped her foot on the floor of the limousine for effect.

Dax laughed. "Is that jealousy I hear, Cassie Kennedy?" Her cheeks reddened and he leaned over and caressed her face. "Don't be embarrassed," he said. "I like it."

"Don't change the subject." She scrunched up her nose. "Does she know you're with me right now?"

He laughed. "Right. Back to the interrogation. Vanessa knows where I am, yes. She always knew this day would come. I hadn't thought about it much to be honest, I haven't exactly been pounding the pavement looking for a relationship. But Vanessa is clear on the arrangement."

"The arrangement?"

He sighed. "I'm going to tell you something I haven't told another soul because it's not my secret to tell. When I do, it becomes your secret too. And, I'm only telling you because you won't trust me until you understand what the nature of my relationship is with Vanessa."

"Okay." She nodded.

"Vanessa is a lesbian."

Cassie's eyes widened. "Well, unless you have a bigger secret of your own to tell me," she said, pointing a finger at him. "I'm not sure how many more secrets I can be responsible for keeping tonight. But why is she following you around like a lovesick puppy? And before you answer that, I know what I felt last week, buddy." She nodded towards his pants. "So, if you were born a woman, you must have one hell of a surgeon."

Dax threw his head back and laughed. "You really are something else. Definitely not the standard issue." He wiped at the corner of his eyes. "I assure you I am one hundred percent male." She looked at him out the corner of her eye and they both laughed.

"So, what does this have to do with you?" Cassie asked.

"Vanessa's been in a long-term relationship for a few years now with a great woman. But not everyone in her life would be okay with this."

Cassie nodded slowly. "Generally, people have become more accepting in Ireland. Is that not the case here?"

"Generally—yes. But she doesn't think her father Franklin Roberts, a Fortune 500 mogul, staunch Catholic and politician in the making would be." He shrugged. "She feels she can't come out to her parents right now. Maybe ever. We go to charity dinners and business events she attends on behalf of the family. Like tonight."

Cassie wrinkled her brow. "Nobody should have to justify who they love. But you're both lying. Doesn't that bother either of you?"

"Franklin thinks of me like a second son and I've only ever wanted to help her." A faraway look crossed his handsome face. "Zander's family has been good to me and I owe them a lot. Everything." His tone became serious. "Vanessa needed me and I filled that role. After all they have done for me, I'd do anything for them. But the arrangement was never designed to deny me my own happiness, which hadn't been an issue until now."

"Why now?" Cassie searched his face, seeing a sliver of seriousness and pain clouding his eyes.

His features softened. "Because of you. Vanessa is hardly going to deny me my own happiness after all I've done to preserve hers."

She stared into his deep blue eyes. "Kiss me," she said with a boldness she'd never known.

"No." He shook his head.

Nothing like knocking her straight back to reality. So

much for taking matters into her own hands. She straightened in the seat and pulled her hand from his. It had been a long time since she'd seduced a man and she was obviously out of practice.

"Not so fast," he said, reaching around her. He slid her across the seat so she was nearly on his lap. "I'm going to kiss you, Cassie. But when I do, I'm not stopping. So, let's not start something here we can't finish."

Cassie sucked a slow breath into her lungs. A dull ache crept between her thighs. The car came to a stop outside her building and she waited as Dax opened her door. He said something to the driver, but Cassie didn't catch it. She walked toward the building and in a second he was beside her, his hand lodged at the small of her back, claiming, possessive, as Charlie opened the doors to let them inside.

"How was your evening, Miss Kennedy?" he asked.

"It was lovely, Charlie, thank you." She glanced at Dax. "This is my um—Dax."

Dax stuck his hand out to shake Charlie's. "Dax Carter, friend of Cassie's. Nice to meet you."

"Likewise," Charlie said, crossing the foyer to push the elevator button. "Enjoy the rest of your evening Miss Kennedy, Mr. Carter." He tipped his hat.

Dear God. What must Charlie think of her bringing home a man after only four days in this city? *Jesus, he's your doorman, not your father.* They stood next to each other, not touching. Electricity crackled in the air, but they rode to her floor in silence. The doors opened and Cassie grabbed her key from her clutch as she headed toward her apartment with Dax in tow.

They stepped inside the dark apartment and she hoped he wouldn't trip on the boxes she hadn't unpacked yet. A beam of moonlight shone through the window, casting a faint glow. She scanned the room and found him leaning against a wall, watching her. The look on his face was enough to make her gasp.

"I've been dreaming about this moment all night," he said. Cassie's breath hitched in her throat. Dax's powerful frame took up the whole hallway and she locked eyes with him. "Come here."

As she stepped toward him, he reached for her, pulling her close and wrapping his arms around her. "I'm going to kiss you now."

"Okay."

"Oh, and Cassie?"

"Yeah?"

"That lovely evening you had, it's not over yet." Her quiet gasp was lost as his mouth urgently met hers. Her knees weakened and she was barely able to stand. Dax picked her up and carried her down the hall.

"This one," she said between frantic kisses. She tapped the door and he opened it with one hand, the other firmly planted on her ass as she straddled him.

He set her down and walked them toward her bed, continuing to kiss her in the process. He placed her on her back and lay down beside her, caressing her face. She turned on her side to face him. "Can I have you tonight, Cassie?"

"Yes." She'd wasted enough time in her life. No more regrets.

CHAPTER 9

HIS LIPS SLID ALONG HER NECK, TO HER JAWLINE, lingering on her collarbone as his hand rested on the curve of her hip. Desperate to taste him, Cassie ran her fingers through his hair, pulling him toward her, cradling his face as she captured his mouth with her own. His tongue dipped inside with delicious strokes sending a direct line of heat straight to her clit.

Dax groaned into her mouth as his hand slid up her side and around her back, deftly gliding down the dress's zipper. He slid the fabric off her shoulder, freeing one of her breasts. Taking the nub in his mouth, he flicked it back and forth until she gasped.

"Dax," she hissed between her teeth.

"Do you want me to stop?" he asked, kissing her senseless.

"No." Her hands slid up the front of his dress shirt, searching for the hard chest underneath. "I need to feel you." He helped her by shrugging the tuxedo jacket off shoulder by shoulder and she fumbled at the buttons of his dress shirt. She craved the feel of his skin against hers.

As if sensing her impatience, Dax grabbed the two ends of his shirt and ripped the garment open, the last of the buttons landing somewhere between the bed and the floor. In the time it took Cassie to laugh, his dress shirt was off and he pulled the white undershirt over his head. He tossed it behind him, uncovering the sculpted lines of his stomach.

"Better?" His lips moved to her neck.

"Getting there." She reached for the fly of his pants. He flipped her on her back as she squealed and his hand slid up her thigh, his fingers grazing the silk of her drenched panties.

He dipped a finger inside. "You're so wet," he said in her ear. Cassie shuddered at the promise of his touch. His fingers slid languidly up and down her slit until Cassie arched toward him. Frantic, she grabbed his waist, reaching for his pants again. This time he didn't stop her.

As she bucked against him, the feel of him rock hard against her thigh filled her with excitement. She slid his pants down, splaying a hand down over his hard ass. With her other hand, she freed his erection, caressing it root to tip. Dax blew out a slow breath and she caught his bottom lip with her teeth, before she opened her mouth, letting him inside.

His tongue stroked slowly over hers as his fingers slid back and forth along her slick folds. He rubbed his thumb in slow circles around the raised nub of flesh that begged to be rubbed. Everything about the way Dax touched her, his skilled hands deliberately torturous, turned her on. Her body connected with his in ways she never had with Rhys and she realized what she'd have missed out on had she gone through with the marriage. As the first wave of orgasm washed over her, Cassie cried out, her back arching up to meet him.

"Cassie, I need to have you, now." Dax met her mid-arch. "In that dress."

"Yes," she nodded.

He pulled off his pants, digging his wallet out of the pocket, and she heard the tear of the foil packet. She licked her lips and leaned back as he expertly rolled the condom down over his hard length. He was an impressive size and as she lay there a violent shiver of arousal coursed through her. She'd never achieved a vaginal orgasm with Rhys, but as she lay under this intriguing man, who set all her nerve endings on fire, she wondered if that was about to change.

Cassie spread her legs as Dax hovered over her entry and gently caressed her clit with the head of his cock. "Yes," she whispered as he teased her, the pressure building once again. Unable to stand it, she grabbed him, thrusting him inside her, crying out.

A guttural groan tore from his throat. "Christ, Cassie… you feel so good," he said as he thrust again.

"Don't be gentle." She grabbed his hips, taking more of him inside her.

"Ah…easy, Cassie." He groaned. "I'm no better than a school boy here tonight. You keep that up and I'm going to go."

"So, go." She kissed him hard. "You promised me all night." Cassie lost all sense of time and space, letting nothing but pure instinct guide her. Dax buried his face in her neck, kissing, licking, sucking. Her core tensed violently and her limbs threatened to shake as the next wave pulsed through her. As a small whimper escaped her lips, Dax lifted one of her legs, fixing it over his shoulder, angling her so he could drive deeper. She looked up into the eyes of the man responsible for her undoing and the raw look on his face was the most erotic thing she'd ever seen.

"Dax!" She climaxed in a rush and yelled his name. He

quickened his pace, his hips pumping as he came long and hard.

"Ah, Cassie." As her name fell from his lips he leaned down and kissed her, slow and sweet. When he finally pulled out of her she was weightless and saddened by the loss of their connection. "I'll be right back," he said. He slipped from the bed and padded across her bedroom floor into the small ensuite.

While Dax cleaned himself up, Cassie grabbed a silk nightie from the chair next to the bed. She wiggled out of the dress Jade had lent her and laid it on the back of the chair. As she slipped the nightie over her head, she wondered what the girl would say if she knew all the wicked things that had happened to her in that dress. Nowhere in the rules had Jade said she couldn't have sex in it. She lay back on the bed and chuckled. When Dax returned, he lay down next to her and stroked her hair, placing a chaste kiss on her mouth. He gathered her in his arms and held her as she sighed.

"That was as amazing as I thought it was going to be," she said with a sigh. A lazy grin spread across her face.

"You've given this some thought, have you?" His tone was teasing.

"You haven't?" She leaned her head back to look up at him.

"Only every day, about twenty times a day since I first set eyes on you." He smiled and kissed her forehead. "If I close my eyes, are you going to leave me in the middle of the night again?" he asked.

"Of course not." She leaned up and kissed him full on the mouth. "You're in my apartment."

"Cheeky," he said, tightening his arms around her.

"Hey," she said. "I can hardly breathe."

"Just making sure you'll still be here when I wake up."

"Does this mean you're spending the night?"

"Try to stop me."

Early morning light poured into the bedroom and Cassie rolled over lazily, pulling the sheet with her. She reached for the hard body, whose limbs were intertwined with hers half the night, surprised when her hand ran over a cold, empty sheet. Propping up on her side, she scanned the room for any sign of him, but his clothes were gone. Instead of the Catholic guilt she expected to hit her over the head like a two-by-four, she had a momentary sense of panic. This wasn't a revenge move, was it? She was ashamed by the thought. Dax would never do something so childish. No, that was a Rhys move.

She picked up the pillow he'd used and hugged it close, breathing deep. His scent and the dull ache between her legs were the only remnants of their night together. She thought about the wickedly pleasurable things he'd repeatedly done to her body. Dax used his tongue like a weapon and the memory set her face on fire.

She grabbed her iPhone propped upright against a lamp on the bed night stand and thumbed the home button. Her message screen indicated one unread text and she couldn't ignore the tingling in her belly. She'd be disappointed if it wasn't Dax. She tapped the white message bubble and smiled.

DC: Good morning, beautiful. I regret leaving you in that big bed by yourself. I envisioned creative ways of waking you up this morning, but something came up. xo D

If she could have hugged the phone she would've. She had a few creative ideas of her own to wake him up, but she'd save them for next time. She lay back against her pillow and sighed. The man was insatiable last night and she was no better. She couldn't get enough of him. She preferred to lie here and daydream about him all day, but it was time to haul her ass out of bed and get ready for work.

As she rubbed body wash all over herself, she was reminded of Dax's roaming hands. Touching, caressing, possessing. Her stomach looped a few times at the thought of seeing him later today. She didn't think anyone at work had noticed they'd left the museum together. She'd been discreet when she picked up her purse and said goodnight. Unable to wipe the grin off her face, she wrapped a plush terry cloth robe around her and padded to the kitchen to make coffee. Sitting at the island of her small kitchen she smothered a slice of toast with jam, poured a coffee and turned the morning news on. This was her routine now. Her New York City routine and so far, she loved it.

Humming to herself, she picked up her phone and chewed her lip a minute, contemplating. She could invite him over tonight for dinner. She loved to cook. Cassie started typing when a message popped up on her phone from Siobhan.

SO: Well, haven't you caused quite a stir?

Underneath the message was a link. Frowning, Cassie clicked it, entering an online New York gossip blog called *The Dirt.* The blog post covered the New York Museum of Natural History's shindig last night, complete with photos of the city's elite. Her eyes stopped on one of her and Dax dancing. If she'd ever doubted his interest in her, one look at his face and the heat in his eyes told her everything she needed to know.

Another captured them leaving, his hand low on her back, guiding her into the limousine. The article went on to speculate who this new girl in Dax Carter's life was and mused about a possible split from his long-time girlfriend, and heir to the Roberts' family throne, Vanessa Roberts. Sources confirmed Ms. Roberts had accompanied him to the event at the Metropolitan Museum of Natural History and was inside when he left with the mystery girl. The article pointedly moved into questioning her character. What really caught her eye was 'the other woman'—captioned in bold letters which resembled cut-out magazine letters of various shapes and colours a teenager might use when scrapbooking.

Cassie's heart thumped hard in her chest.

Oh shit.

CHAPTER 10

As she walked to work, Cassie worried about the fallout from the blog. The story had placed her in an untenable situation. How could she possibly defend herself? She believed Dax when he said there was nothing between he and Vanessa. She also understood the situation he was in though she didn't like it. But no one else knew the real story. No one else *could*. She couldn't prove she wasn't a hussy and she wasn't responsible for breaking up a fictitious relationship without outing Vanessa. Cassie couldn't do that because she'd be outing Dax too, in an entirely different way. Either way, she was stuck.

Texting and walking weren't her strong suit, but she took out her phone and messaged Siobhan.

CK: Nobody reads sites like *The Dirt,* do they?

After a few minutes, Siobhan sent her back the "laugh out loud" emoji, which wasn't helpful in the least. The last thing Cassie needed was a scandal. It was bad enough everyone in Kilkenny knew Rhys had cheated on her. A few had also known he'd been doing it a long time. Bastards. Cassie was three thousand miles away from all that shite now and she was happy with her new life. She didn't need any more drama.

She also had no idea if she and Dax would be anything to each other beyond this week, but she was willing to find out. She deserved a shot at some happiness. Lord knew she'd had enough heartache to last a lifetime. It was time to throw caution to the wind. Dax was a great distraction. She was only having a little fun, right? If she kept telling herself that she might believe it. Deep down, she knew if she wasn't careful she could fall for Dax. Hard. She wondered if he'd seen the article. She opened the screen and re-read his message. She needed to test the waters.

CK: Good morning, handsome.

She waited for the response dots, but none appeared. The closer she got to the Franklin Building the more the jitters set in. She scanned the lobby, hoping not to bump into any of her colleagues. The two girls on the front desk in the foyer of Crave stared at her a little longer than necessary this morning, considering they usually ignored her. She shook the thought from her head. She was overreacting. *Wait till I get my hands on you Siobhan O'Mara. An eternal curse on your love life for sending me that link!* She opened her computer screen and was scanning through her email, when Serena popped her head in.

"Good morning, Cassie."

"Oh hey, Serena. How are you? Good time last night?" Cassie babbled, the nervousness kicking into high gear. Perhaps the girl wouldn't notice.

"Yeah, great. You okay?" The girl raised her eyebrows.

"Oh, yes, sure." Every person who walked by Cassie's office cast a glance backwards and her paranoia was fast approaching the breaking point.

"Early night?" Serena asked, a playful edge to her voice.

Cassie noted the hint of a smile forming on Serena's lips. "Ugh," Cassie threw her head in her hands. "Does everyone know?"

Serena closed the door and walked over to Cassie's desk, plopping down in a sleek chair. "Know what?" Her eyes twinkled with mischief and she laughed. "Okay. Gina has a Google Alert set up on Mr. Carter because she's obsessed with him. She got *The Dirt's* blog post first thing this morning. So, the short answer is, yes. Most of us know."

Sacred heart of Mary.

"Well, I don't think they know in the mail room, yet." Serena laughed. "Gina is pissed, of course. If Mr. Carter were going to cheat on Ms. Roberts, she can't understand why it couldn't have been with her." She reached over to pat Cassie's hand. "But don't worry. She'll get over it."

"He's not ch—" Cassie stopped. She couldn't say what she wanted to. "This is not how I wanted my first week at Crave to go." Gina Lombardi's fascination with Dax was the farthest thing from Cassie's mind. But she needed to talk to Dax. Maybe he could fix this.

"Listen, Cassie, we're the least of your worries."

"What's that supposed to mean?"

"I mean you're an adult, so is Mr. Carter. What you two do is your own business and it's not my place to judge." Serena gave her a sympathetic smile. "But I doubt Helen Roberts feels that way and she's going to be in our boardroom in less than a half an hour."

"What?" Cassie jumped to her feet but found it hard to steady herself.

"Hey," Serena said. "Maybe you should sit down, Cassie. You're white as a sheet."

That was hardly surprising. She was filled with confusion and nervousness and frustration. It was like an elevator had left her brain and plummeted straight to her feet in two seconds.

"We have a meeting with the special projects team from the Museum of Natural History this morning." Serena held up her phone. "I got an email from Victor saying that she decided to attend the meeting as well."

"Does she usually do that?"

"Nope. Mrs. Roberts is a heavy-hitting socialite who hosts parties and raises money, but sitting in a board room, brainstorming projects and discussing scope creep isn't exactly her cup of tea."

"Sweet Lord have mercy," Cassie said plopping down in her chair. "Is this about me?"

Serena chewed the side of her lip. "I don't know. But you'd better bring your A-game, girl. Sounds to me like she's coming to check out her daughter's competition."

~

To the unsuspecting and passing eye, Cassie looked perfectly groomed, seated in her office, sipping her coffee, engrossed in work. However, by the time ten o'clock rolled around, she was a hot mess. She'd texted Dax at least five times, all of which had gone unanswered and she was furious. What angered her most is she was bearing the brunt of this all on her own. Gina was ignoring her and people were walking past her office, eying her like she was on display at the circus. One woman, whose name she didn't know, stopped in her doorway and clapped.

To top it all off, in a few minutes, she was expected to face Vanessa's mother in a boardroom. For all she knew the woman would fire her. Technically, she could. Her husband owned the company. Cassie had thought of every scenario from hiding in the ladies' room to pulling the fire alarm.

She'd even had a fleeting thought to come clean and tell Mrs. Roberts the truth about Vanessa and Dax. None were viable options.

She'd go to the meeting. It was her job. With dread weighing her down like a pair of cement shoes, she trudged toward the boardroom. She met Serena and the rest of them as they were entering. As they assembled around, Cassie parked herself as far from the head of the table as possible.

"Is there a creative brief?" Cassie asked Serena, leaning in close.

Serena shook her head. "No, we're not that far along yet. I sent around an email earlier with some of Victor's notes. I'm not up to speed on the project at all, but I gather it's something to do with trying to become more relevant to tweens. Did you read that?"

Cassie shook her head. "No. I was too busy trying to find the fire escape."

Serena chuckled. "Victor is the Special Projects Team Lead with the Museum and he'll be here today. He's fantastic. He has a solid marketing background and speaks our language. He'll explain everything."

The hair on the back of Cassie's neck prickled; she felt Dax's presence before she saw him. His smooth baritone voice was sexy as hell and she couldn't deny what it did to her even though she was livid with him. She'd know his spicy, woodsy smell if she were trapped in a fousty gym locker with a pair of six-week old unwashed football socks. The minute Dax entered a room he owned it. Tight on his tale this morning was a slightly older version of Vanessa. Slight being the operative word.

Obviously, only New York's finest surgeons worked on Helen Roberts. From afar, she was a dead ringer for her daughter. Dressed in the latest trends, slim and well groomed, she scanned the room with precision. Her feline green eyes had raked over Cassie at least twice in a manner of seconds. Cassie knew her type. The woman was a fox and twice as cunning. Several others came into the room behind them and took seats around the table. The staff talked to them with the familiarity of old friends and she assumed they were the Museum's special project's team.

"Good morning," Dax said as the small chat dwindled and they opened their notebooks. "I think most of you know Helen Roberts, Chair of the Board for the Museum of Natural History," he said. The woman nodded dismissively and took a seat to Dax's left.

Cassie held her breath, bracing herself for her own introduction, which he was surely going to do. Everyone in the room had glanced at her at least once. There was no ignoring she was the only new person in attendance. His blue eyes skittered over her and she locked on them for what felt like an eternity. He hesitated, but was back on his game in a nanosecond.

"I'm going to turn things over to Victor now to explain what the museum wants to achieve," Dax continued, nodding at Victor. He unbuttoned his black pinstripe suit coat and took a seat at the head of the boardroom table, next to Vanessa's mother.

Cassie had never been punched in the gut before but the breathless pounding pain deep in her core must be similar. Dax had only left her bed a few hours ago, yet the impersonal glance he shot in her direction was no more than the one he gave anyone else in the room. Her blood boiled and she tried to keep her emotions in check. What did she expect from him exactly? To single her out—throw his arms around her and kiss her in front of the whole room? Heat rose to her cheeks. No, of course, not. But what she wanted was some acknowledgement that he understood her predicament. That she was worth introducing to the people around the table. That none of this was her fault. She wanted some acknowledgment that she wasn't going through this alone. Some acknowledgement that last night meant something. Or had he changed his mind since he left her this morning?

"Hey everybody," Victor said. "Great night last night, thank you all for being there. We're waiting for the final tally to come in, but it looks like we raised over ten million dollars for our youth programs." Victor's voice was drowned out by the chorus of whistling and words of encouragement that followed. "Yeah, it's great. Of course, none of it would be possible without this wonderful lady at the head of the table," he said, gesturing his hand toward Mrs. Roberts, who smiled and nodded, graciously accepting her accolades as a woman well used to the limelight. "And of course, she's also responsible for bringing the amazingly creative people here at Crave to us."

More whistling and excited chatter. Victor was smart. Flattering the folks you needed to pull out a marketing campaign for you definitely couldn't hurt. With her chair strategically pushed back so Serena's body blocked most of her own, Cassie could see a sliver of Dax's face. She searched his eyes and expression as Victor explained what the museum wanted to accomplish. Instead of his chin up, eyes bright and looking confidently around the room for a flicker of creativity on the faces of the people he employed, Dax was slumped in his chair. He was entirely disengaged from the conversation around him and did not make eye contact with her once.

Her spider senses tingled. Eyes other than Dax's sought her out. She tilted her head with one small movement, widened her view, and sure enough found Helen Roberts' cat-like eyes studying her. The room chilled by twenty degrees. Somewhere in the back of her mind it registered that Victor was still talking.

"We want to figure out how to engage with young people so that separate from their class trips they want to come back to the museum. How do we make it relevant to them? We want them to tweet about it and tell their friends on Facebook about it. We also want them to engage with us, but we're not sure how to get them to *want* to do that," he finished.

As the team took notes, Cassie's wheels turned and she was happy for a distraction from the two elephants in the room. She would focus on the work. Creative thinking was her thing.

"First, you need to go where the kids are and it's not Twitter and Facebook. Facebook has pretty much been overtaken by fifty plus women and grandmothers," said Josh.

Seated next to Serena, Cassie felt her kick Josh under the table.

"Oh jeez. I'm sorry," he said, placing his palms in the air as if in surrender mode. "I only meant—it's where ah —" He stammered before regaining his purpose. "Women of a certain *demographic* go to look at pictures of their grandchildren and share them with their friends."

Serena's normally pleasant face twisted in a warning look that demanded he cease and desist.

"No offense Mrs. Roberts." Josh's face flushed.

"None taken," she said.

"Since you're not a grandmother." Dax's eyes never left the woman's face, but his expression was unreadable.

"Yet." She deadpanned. "A mere technicality." She shifted her head wordlessly in Cassie's direction with a cold, measured look that could've turned the boardroom into one full sheet of ice.

Cassie glanced at Dax. The muscle in his jaw had tightened and he shifted in his seat as Helen's cool gaze returned to him. There were expectations in those words. A warning in that look. She cursed him for making her believe there was something between them that could never be. He wasn't in love with Vanessa and they weren't in a real relationship, but this display told Cassie everything she needed to know. The look on the matriarch's face confirmed he was one hundred percent owned by the Roberts Family. Gina had been right all along—Dax Carter was off limits.

Cassie had two options. She could sit in this fancy boardroom for the next hour, hiding behind Serena all morning or she could cut her losses and show them both why she'd been hired by Crave. Hell, show them all she wasn't here because Dax wanted his side-bit down the hall. Above all else Cassie was a Kennedy and that meant she was a survivor. She was also damned good at her job. She pulled her chair into the table and sat up straight, leaning forward with her hands folded in front of her.

"So, where are they?" Victor asked.

"They're on Snapchat and Instagram and—"

"Yes, that's true Josh," Cassie interrupted. "But just because you've identified the platforms kids spend their time on doesn't mean you're any closer to making the museum more relevant to them." Her voice silenced Josh and everyone in the room turned to her, including Dax and Helen. Something flickered in his eyes. Oh yes, Cassie Kennedy had arrived. *Hang onto your pinstripes, Dax Carter.*

She wasted mere seconds returning the same blasé, impersonal glance he'd given her before shifting her gaze and looking directly into the belly of the beast. Every fibre of Cassie's being said that locking eyes with the woman would be like staring directly at the sun during an eclipse.

A couple of seconds passed and Cassie didn't spontaneously combust so she continued. "What you're saying Victor, is you want kids to come to your museum, engage with you on a social media platform, continue to talk about their experience to their friends on that platform, and want to come back for more."

Victor nodded. "Yeah, that about sums it up."

"Do your adult museum-goers do that?" Cassie asked.

"Well, no. I mean, they leave reviews and we get some of them back when there's a new exhibit," Victor said.

"Sure, but you've already got them. They're your repeat cultural clients who will continue to come back because their social and economic backgrounds have made places like museums relevant to them. If you want kids to talk about you after they leave the experience must be something they really connect with," Cassie said.

"We have world-class exhibits directed at students that are interesting and meet curriculum guidelines." Victor narrowed his eyes at Cassie and crossed his arms.

"I'm sure you do. But kids don't care about curriculum guidelines. They aren't going to post a photo on Instagram of an exhibit, linking it to a page in their social studies text book. Where's the fun in that? You need to think outside the box."

"If you have an idea, Ms.—?" The woman trailed off with a question in her tone.

Oh, we're playing the I'm-going-to-pretend-I-don't-know-who-you-are game. Well, game on Granny wannabe.

"Kennedy, Cassie Kennedy. I'm the new MarComm director here at Crave. Nice to meet you." Cassie gave her most winning smile. "And I have plenty of ideas. It's why I was hired."

A smile tugged on the corner of Dax's lips as he twirled a pen between his fingers. Cassie was most assuredly hitting her stride. She might not excel at matters of the heart, but this was her jam. The woman's eyes widened. Hopefully she had enough Botox around her beady eyes to keep them in her head.

"What I'm trying to say is we know that a museum's success has everything to do with visitor experience, right?"

Victor nodded, scrubbing his goatee with one hand.

"So, you need to enhance the visitor experience for youth."

"Okay," he said. "You mean designing new exhibits?"

"I doubt there's anything wrong with your current exhibits," she said. "When you get young people here, I bet they enjoy them and they probably learn from them. But how do they relate to them? How do they soak in the experience and want to share it with their friends?"

"You tell me, Miss Kennedy. Sounds like you might know a lot about this." Victor uncrossed his arms and smiled, all remnants of defensiveness gone.

"As it happens I do." Cassie focussed solely on Victor and flashed him a sweet smile. "So, give them something they can't get anywhere else. Something exclusive and fun. Something memorable. An experience they'll rave about on Instagram."

"Such as?"

Cassie and Victor shot back and forth at each other like a ball at a Wimbledon tennis match. You could almost hear the oohs and aahs as the heads in the room followed suit.

"How about a sleepover at the museum?" Cassie asked.

"I'm not sure I follow."

"All kids love slumber parties, right? The ones in Ireland do. I can't imagine New York youth being all that different. Try some group sleepovers. Girl Guide troops and birthday parties, as a pilot project. Set up some social media channels so they can snapchat and do live video feed from the museum. A night under the stars with Van Gogh. Assign hashtags. You see where I'm going with this?"

A slow smile spread across Victor's lips and he nodded. "I do. I see exactly what you're saying." He pointed his finger in the air. "And I like it."

"We did an outreach program in Dublin a few years ago. Not like this, but it focussed on access to culture. They wanted to get youth from outside the city into the museums and art galleries. It all came down to youth engagement and how they spread the word to their friends through social media. The institutions that took part doubled their youth numbers in two months and their online engagement shot through the roof. I can put you in contact with one of the museum's directors if you'd like to hear more about the success of that program."

"That'd be fantastic." Victor looked at Helen. "It's a great idea, Mrs. Roberts."

She sat back in her chair, hands folded, poker face in place, giving Victor nothing.

"It's obviously up to you to pitch it to the board," he continued. "And we'll need to sort liability and insurance, but I think we could have a lot of fun with this."

"Very clever." Her eyes were set on Cassie.

Deciding to take command of the room as head of the team Cassie said, "I'll have Serena put together a creative brief and we'll set our next meeting for one week from today. The full team will review the direction and feed into the critical path. If that is amenable to you all?"

"Works for me," Victor said, shooting to his feet. He came around the table as Cassie stood. "It's great to meet you, Miss Kennedy. I think this is going to be a great project." He shot her a brilliant smile, hanging onto her hand just a touch too long.

"Call me Cassie," she said withdrawing her hand from

his. "I think so too. I'm going to leave you and Serena to toss around some dates for the next meeting." She couldn't stay in this room with Dax any longer. She glanced in Helen's direction. "Very nice to meet you Mrs. Roberts. I look forward to seeing what we can do to help the museum increase its youth engagement and your visitation."

Cassie stood, signalling the meeting's end, and slipped out the side door of the boardroom. As she closed it behind her, she heaved a long sigh. Jesus, that was hard. Pulling herself together, she headed in the direction of her office.

"Cassie, wait." A hand tugged on her arm and she whipped around to face those piercing blue eyes. "Listen, I just wanted to say thanks."

"For what? Doing my job?" She raised her eyebrows and stared at him.

"No, I mean you could have made that difficult for me. And you didn't." His eyes softened as he spoke and he stroked her arm.

"Go to hell Dax." She shrugged free from his grasp and walked away, holding back the tears.

CHAPTER 11

DAX PACED BACK AND FORTH IN HIS SPACIOUS OFFICE, TWO floors up from Cassie's. After all he'd done to help Vanessa over the years he couldn't believe she'd throw him to the wolves. He hadn't had a shred of happiness in years. Now, he'd met Cassie, an amazing woman, and Vanessa refused to let him out of their agreement.

"Hey." Zander poked his head in Dax's office. "I'm here for a meeting with finance and thought I'd stop by. How goes it?"

"Just fucking great," Dax said.

Zander's eyes widened and he stepped inside Dax's office, closing the door behind him. "You look terrible. Everything okay?"

"What do you think? Jesus Christ man, you've got to help me talk some sense into your sister before I lose any shot I ever had at Cassie."

"What do you mean? I saw you leave with her last night. I assumed…well, you know?"

"Yeah, well the night was going great until your sister called me, hysterical because some stupid online blogger insinuated that I dumped the 'heiress Roberts.'" Dax used air quotes around her name. "For a Jenny-from-the-block-girl. She called me at four this morning and made me go over to the penthouse. And guess who was there?"

"Don't say it." Zander covered his ears.

"Oh yes."

"Wow. Ness must be awfully pissed at you if she called in the big guns." Zander shuddered. "I've made my peace with never getting married because of her. I can't bring myself to inflict Helen on any woman, but especially not one I care about."

"Yes, well, Helen was pretty clear about her expectations regarding me and Vanessa. It also didn't take her long to throw everything in my face, reminding me how much your family has done to help. As if I don't know. As if I don't thank God every day for your kindness." Dax stopped ranting and rested against a steel grey credenza behind his desk. He pinched the bridge of his nose. "You've got to talk some sense into your sister."

"Dax, man, Ness is a pretty tough nut to crack. She knows Franklin would go ballistic over this. He'd probably cut her off."

Dax had always gotten a kick out of the way Zander referred to his parents by their given names. Today, he couldn't give a shit.

"Are you kidding me? I've seen the way he looks at her." Dax paced behind his desk. "He adores her. He's not cutting her off. He wants to turn the keys to the empire over to her. No offence, but you know it's true."

"None taken." Zander shrugged. "Vanessa has always been the brains and believe me, I know my limitations. As for Franklin, I love the guy, but he's as homophobic as they come. And he'll be mad as hell at you too for lying to him."

"This can't be happening," Dax said. "I'm going to lose her before she's really mine to lose."

"I'm sorry man."

"Listen Zander, I need a few Roberts-free minutes, if you don't mind. I know none of this is your fault, but your family has got me feeling a little crazy right now." More to the point, he needed a few minutes to consider how he was going to get through to Cassie. Vanessa wasn't thinking straight right now out of fear. But he hoped after she'd had a few days to mull it over, she'd come around. She had to. His happiness depended on it.

"Yeah, no problem, I got to run anyway. Why don't we hit Oasis Saturday night? I know a night on the town won't fix everything, but some smoking hot ladies and a little music might make you feel a bit better, for a while." Zander shot Dax a boyish grin. "What do you say?"

Dax heaved a sigh. "Yeah, sure."

"All right." Zander clapped his hands. "I'll round up the boys. Catch you later, Dax."

"Later." He only had one smoking hot lady on his mind right now and that was Cassie Kennedy.

Too bad she thought he was the scum of the earth.

~

"We are most definitely going out tonight, Cassie. It's your thirtieth birthday, it's Saturday night and we're in New York City for God's sake. I'm not going to let you sit inside and rot like a spinster, as much as you want to," Siobhan said. "Next thing you'll be living with thirty-five cats and knitting socks for them all night. No way, Kennedy. And besides I've got a surprise."

"Plus, it's my last night here! We have to go out." Scarlett clinked her glass with Siobhan's and tipped it on its head.

"I hate your surprises," Cassie said. "Historically, they never work out well for me. And by the way, that's not entirely fair." She walked out of the kitchen with her hands on her hips. "I've tried hard since I got here to put Rhys behind me and move on. I don't know why, but I seem to pick the bad ones."

"I'll give you that. Rhys was a bollix, all right, but we all saw that a country mile off, right?" Siobhan looked from Scarlett to Cassie, whose mouth widened in protest. "Okay, we've established you did not. Fair play." Siobhan shrugged. "But truly, I thought you might have nailed it with blue eyes. I mean what a ride he is." She picked up a set of chopsticks and expertly lifted a piece of sushi from a container on Cassie's coffee table. "I'll admit I never saw this coming. Who knew he'd turn out to be such a shitehawk?" She stuffed the sushi in her mouth and reached for her wine. "Anyway, we're going out. There's no more discussion. Throw on that slinky black number I brought over and your Lous, whack on a bit of smack and we'll be good to go." Siobhan winked at Scarlett.

Cassie grumbled, heading toward her bedroom. "I draw the line at strippers," she called over her shoulder.

"You're seriously no fun," Siobhan said.

A few hours later, Cassie found herself dragged past a line-up of scantily clad females at least a mile long. According to Siobhan, who had done some HR work for the club's owner, Oasis was one of the hottest night clubs on the New York party scene and Siobhan had a standing "get in free" card. It also didn't hurt that she was gorgeous and all legs in a shimmery shirt-dress, barely covering her ass. She was an unobtainable vision that nearly brought the male bouncers to their knees and they waved the three of them inside to the protests of many, who claimed to have been in this line all night.

Siobhan led them through a sea of people and up to the second floor where several of her colleagues from Crave gathered on couches and chairs, in a sexy sitting area, complete with black leather couches and soft purplish light to the left of the dance floor. Looking up from a deep conversation with Luke, Serena waved, and stood to meet them. Cassie looked at Siobhan and Scarlett, her mouth open wide.

"Surprise!" Scarlett yelled.

"Hey Cassie, happy birthday." Serena leaned in to hug her. One by one, Josh, Luke, Portia, Cara, and Cristal came forward and gave her a birthday hug.

"Girl, let me get a look at you." Josh swung her around by one hand. "You are hot tonight." He kissed her on both cheeks. "If only you were my type." He placed a hand over his heart, and cocked his head to the side, a wistful look passing over his face.

"Wow, you're all here. Thank you, guys. That means a lot." For the first time since yesterday morning, a spark of happiness shot through Cassie. She turned around looking for Siobhan, who was studying something on her phone. She'd been checking her phone all night, making Cassie wonder what else the girl had up her sleeve. "Hey, Shi?"

"Yeah, babe?" Siobhan looked up from her screen.

"Thanks for this."

Siobhan shot her an air kiss. "Anything for my girl. And the night is only young." She flashed a wicked smile. "More surprises to come!"

Dear God.

A server appeared with a tray of drinks and Cassie accepted a fruity cocktail of some concoction. As she sipped through the straw, she scanned the club. The bar was sleek and attractive much like the patrons who filled the place. The massive dance floor was the focal point and around its perimeter was a staircase in each corner, leading to the next level. A long bar ran one full side of the second floor and a quick look at the bar staff told Cassie that a prerequisite to working here or drinking here was beauty. There were more beautiful people in this square footage than in the whole of Kilkenny, she thought. On the dance floor, bodies were stacked against each other writhing to the rhythm of the music.

As she alternated between studying the dancers below and the couples sitting close on the couches around her, thoughts of Dax crept into her mind. She tried to shake them and her gaze landed back on her colleagues again. Josh had everyone enthralled with a story about a client, who wanted him to wear an elephant costume. As they laughed comfortably with one another, her heart filled. They'd all turned up on a Saturday night to celebrate her birthday. She'd only known them a week, but she got the impression they were a loyal bunch. Though she'd gotten that impression from Dax too. And how wrong she was about that.

They shared a strong connection, she couldn't deny it. But she also couldn't go down this road. A gossip rag had already labeled her the "other woman." Helen Roberts' visit to the boardroom screamed—hands off! It didn't matter that Cassie knew they weren't cheaters. You couldn't be labeled a cheater when there was no relationship. But no one else knew that. Besides, she couldn't share him. Eventually Vanessa's needs would clash with her own and where would that leave her? No, it was a disaster waiting to happen. Too complicated. Call it bad timing, but she couldn't mean that much to him if he'd rather keep a pretend relationship over a real one. A surprising pang of sadness washed over her, as she realized the cons far outweighed her heart's desire.

"Come on Cassie, let's hit the dance floor." Scarlett grabbed her by the hand.

"Great idea." Josh danced between them. "I'm coming too."

"Hang on." Cassie laid her drink on a side table near her friends as Scarlett and Josh dragged her behind them. As they pushed their way onto the dance floor she said, "I'm entirely far too sober for this yet, Scar."

"Throw caution to the wind, Cassie." Scarlett gave into the music, shaking her ass and moving to the beat. "We're in a room full of strangers and I'm leaving tomorrow. Let's party."

As Josh danced, the two of them stared open-mouthed. The boy had rhythm. "You put everyone to shame out here!" Cassie yelled over the music.

"I know, girlfriend." He slipped into a Bruno Mars's *Uptown Funk* dance impression. "Even my moves have moves." As he danced away from her Cassie laughed and shook her head at her colleague and newfound friend.

Scarlett was right. Where was the harm in breaking loose and having a little fun? Song after song the three of them danced. Cassie forgot about Dax and Rhys, losing herself in the music. It was therapeutic. Several men approached them eager to pair off, but Cassie and Scarlett waved them away, happy enough to dance with Josh. Siobhan and Scarlett always had her best interests at heart and she was glad they made her come out even though the events of the last week had gotten her down.

The music finally slowed and the crowd collapsed into couples. That was Cassie's cue. She put a hand on Scarlett's shoulder, indicating she should stay and dance with Josh. She'd almost made it off the dance floor when a hand caressed a long stroke down her arm and clasped her hand. It sent a shiver to her core and Cassie spun around, looking up into a set of piercing blue eyes.

"Stay, please," Dax said. "I've been watching you all night, trying to muster up the courage to come talk to you."

"You suddenly need courage to talk to me? You didn't need much courage to land in my bed."

Something flickered in his eyes. "Okay, I deserved that." He held her hand between his and kissed it."Dance with me."

She scanned the room for Scarlett and Josh, but they were lost to the floor.

When she didn't move, he took it as a sign and pulled her closer, one hand resting against the curve of her back. "You look amazing."

"Thanks."

"You didn't answer any of my texts," he said.

"How does that feel?"

He closed his eyes. "I know. The situation is—"

"Not my problem," she finished. She wasn't sure how she was mustering this coldness. It wasn't like her to be abrasive. Perhaps Rhys's actions had impacted her more than she'd realized.

"I want it to be your problem." He slid his hands around her waist, pulling her close. "I know what you're thinking.

"Do you?"

"I'm not fucking you around Cassie. At least, I'm not trying to."

"You have a bizarre way of showing it." She searched his eyes and what she saw there scared her. He wasn't lying, but she was no less confused by his behaviour.

"I know. It's complicated. Vanessa's reaction is not

what I expected." Dax frowned. Cassie noticed the dark circles around his eyes.

"You look tired."

"I haven't slept much since I left your place Thursday night."

"So instead of staying home to get some rest you're out on the prowl?" She caressed his cheek.

"What? No. Not on the prowl. Zander always thinks the answer to heartache is a night on the town."

"Your heart is aching?" Cassie leaned her body back and tilted her head to look up at him. Dax tightened his arms around her.

"My heart's going to ache until you forgive me."

She wanted nothing more than to forgive him. This attractive man holding her tight, pouring his heart out, was sexy as hell. And she wanted him. But he had power. Power to hurt her. Power to break her heart if she let him get too close. And he was already too close.

"And what about you? Are you on the prowl?"

She laughed. "Me? Ah no. Have you learned anything about me yet? I assure you wherever in God's creation Siobhan is tonight, that woman is most assuredly on the prowl. But much to her chagrin—I don't prowl."

"I'd love to learn everything about you." He brushed his lips along her jaw line.

A shiver of pleasure washed over her. "Okay. Well let's start with the basics. I'm only out tonight because Siobhan and Scarlett made me."

"So, you're an unwilling participant." Dax fluttered kisses along her neck.

Her knees weakened a little, but his hand at the small of her back tightened.

"Kind of. But it's my birthday."

"It's your birthday?" He stopped his slow decline of his

mouth and met her eyes. "Oh, Cassie, why didn't you tell me your birthday was today?"

"I didn't get much of a chance to tell you anything. Besides, what would it matter? It doesn't change your situation."

His eyes flickered something. Guilt? Regret? Sadness? All of the above.

"Cassie, let me handle Vanessa. She will come around, I promise you that. I need to give her some time to get used to the idea."

Cassie worried her bottom lip, unable to break his gaze.

"I don't want to walk away. Tell me you feel it too." He searched her eyes.

"Of course, I feel something," she said. "And it scares me. It scares me a lot. I moved my whole life here after a terrible breakup. I thought I was going to spend the rest of my life with Rhys. I was prepared to. About to say I do. And…" she trailed off. "I need this. This fresh start in New York, and I need this job and these people." She gestured around with her hands and dropped her gaze.

He gently lifted her chin up, forcing her to look at him. "Why do your feelings scare you?"

"They scare me—" she stopped. "Because I feel more for you already than I ever felt for Rhys in five years. And that's just—it's too soon." She pulled away from him. "You have the power to hurt me, Dax. And I don't think I can handle that." Her eyes brimmed, but she willed the tears away. "So, if you know you're going to break my heart—do it now. But don't prolong my agony." She stared into his heated blue eyes.

"I'll never break your heart, Cassie," he said, lowering his mouth to hers. "Not without shattering my own." He kissed her ferociously, his hands wandering her body. When they finally pulled apart he said, "Let's get out of here and celebrate your birthday properly."

"I don't know." She bit the side of her lip.

"Please, Cassie. Let me make up the last few days to you." He kissed her again. "Let me show you how sorry I am." His lips brushed her neck and she shivered.

"All right." She pulled back and wagged her finger in his face. "But you have a lot of making up to do."

"Is that a challenge?" He pulled her in tight, his hands roaming her back. "Cause I'm up for it."

She laughed, wiggling free from his hold. "I'm just going to say goodbye to everyone. I'll meet you out front." Cassie followed him off the dance floor, casting her eyes around for her friends.

"I'll be waiting for you." Dax pulled her against him for another searing kiss before letting her go.

When he released her Cassie was breathless. Composing herself she resumed her search and found Scarlett perched on the arm of a couch, drink in one hand, phone in the other.

"Hey Scar," Cassie said. "Where is everyone?"

"I have no idea. I'm just waiting for Josh to hit the floor again. He's a machine!" She sipped through the straw. "Was that Dax you were with a few minutes ago?" Scarlett asked with wide eyes.

Cassie nodded.

"He is dreamy."

Cassie laughed. "He sure is. Listen, would you forgive me if I cut out a little early?" She wrinkled her nose and squinted at her childhood friend.

"Of course not." Scarlett pretended to swoon, flapping her hand in front of her face. "Happy birthday to you!" She jumped up and enveloped Cassie in a tight hug. "I'll be back for a conference in February so I'll see you soon." Scarlett kissed her on the cheek.

"Have a safe flight and text me when you're home safe and sound," Cassie said.

"Will do."

"Tell everyone I said good night, ok? I'm so happy they all came out."

"Have fun!" Scarlett said with a mischievous glint in her eye.

The valet brought Dax's Mercedes to a side door of Oasis. Dax helped her inside before jogging around the front of the car and sliding into the driver's seat. There was something about the smell of the black leather seats and the overwhelming scent of Dax. The way he ran his hand up her leg turned Cassie on. In an instant, her panties were soaked.

"You call this a dress?" He removed his hand from her thigh to shift gears and pull away from the curb.

Cassie's skin burned from his touch. "Like it?" She shot him a side-glance, her eyes locking onto his.

"I'll like it better on the floor." The look he gave her was pure unadulterated lust.

"Promises, promises," she teased, suddenly conscious of how short her dress was. She reached for the hem and pulled.

Dax chuckled. "Too late for modesty now, honey. The whole time you were dancing all I could think was—I know what's under that dress." His hand caressed the inner curve of her thigh. "And I want more of it."

Cassie gasped. If he got any closer he'd find the drenched underwear and the source underneath. Oh, holy God.

Too late.

"Fuck, Cassie." He growled. The car suddenly veered

right as he pulled into the parking lot of an abandoned building. The car jerked to a stop and in seconds he was out of his seatbelt and had unbuckled hers. He pulled her into his lap, maneuvering her legs to either side of his.

"Dax!" She laughed, struggling to catch up to his sudden movements. He silenced her with a penetrating kiss she felt in her toes. As one hand tangled in her hair, at the base of her neck, his other snaked between her legs. He pushed her panties aside and plunged two fingers deep inside and she cried out.

"Dear God." Cassie saw stars as he stroked her. She moaned, her head falling forward and she nipped at his shoulder with her teeth.

"I need you now."

His fingers found what they were looking for, what she craved. She shuddered and tightened around his hand. She unbuttoned his pants freeing his erection. He produced a packet and she grabbed it from his hands. She took great pleasure in stroking his hard length as she rolled the condom on. He shuddered at her touch.

"Jesus Christ," he whispered before claiming her tongue. As he teased and stroked her opening she sat up on her knees and he angled his cock toward her. His eyes opened and the heat emanating from them was enough to melt the leather seats. Staring into the depths of his blue eyes she plunged down on him without stopping, taking him right to her core. The sudden movement caused them both to cry out.

"Fuck, Cassie. You feel so good." His head rolled back against the seat.

Her hands came to rest on either side of his face.

"Look at me," she said, quickening her pace.

"Look at you? Cassie, you're the only thing I see."

CHAPTER 12

CASSIE WOKE TO THE AROMA OF BACON AND COFFEE. AND A warm body snuggled against her. After two failed attempts, she and Dax had finally spent a full night in bed together. Sleeping wasn't high on the agenda. A lazy smile spread across her face. That man. But if Dax was lying next to her, who the hell was in her kitchen? Scarlett had an early flight back to Dublin. Had someone broken in? She thought about all Nana's warnings. What kind of a burglar cooked breakfast for the people he robbed?

Cassie slid out from under Dax's arm and reached for a silk robe on a nearby chair. Wrapping it tight around her, she warily crept down the hall toward the kitchen. A slow smile spread across her face. She leaned against the wall and observed the ink-covered arms expertly flipping pancakes in her kitchen, their owner humming to himself. Just like home.

"And what do you think you're doing in my kitchen?" Cassie asked.

With a pan in one hand and a spatula in the other, her younger brother, Colm, flashed one of his playful grins.

"Good mornin', Sis. What time of the day do you call this?"

Cassie rushed into the kitchen and he laid down his cooking utensils and scooped her up into a big bear hug. He kissed both her cheeks before setting her down again.

"What are you doing here?"

"I thought I'd come and see how you're faring in the Big Apple. Your Nanna is nearly gone thinking about all the terrible things that are going to happen to you here. I said, 'Don't worry Nanna, I've got it under control.'" He kissed her on the forehead. "And I may have missed you this much." He held his forefinger and thumb close together and squinted in jest. "But I'll deny it if you tell anyone. I have my reputation to uphold as a bad ass."

She playfully punched his arm. "But what about the band? Tommy's not going to want you gone for long."

"Yeah, we're good. It's fine. I thought maybe I'd scope out the scene here, make a few connections." He shrugged. "If it works out the lads can come over and we'll play a few gigs here. Expand our horizons, you know?"

"When did you—"

"Well, I see you finally found your birthday surprise." Siobhan came up behind Cassie in nothing but a t-shirt barely covering her ass.

A black t-shirt. A signature wardrobe staple of Colm's. Since he was currently shirtless, and the shirt was at least two sizes too big for Siobhan, Cassie was going to go out on a limb and make a sweeping generalization that Siobhan was wearing Colm's shirt. In fact, she was going to go one step further and surmise that Siobhan was fully responsible for taking it off him too.

"You tore out of the club with lover boy so fast last night you didn't stick around for the grand finale. Surprise." She flashed jazz hands in a failed attempt at humour. Siobhan slid around a wide-eyed Cassie and stepped into the kitchen. She reached into the cupboard for a mug and Colm lifted a piece of crispy bacon from his stash and carefully placed it between her lips. The look that passed between her best friend and brother could have fried the bacon. Cassie tightened the belt on her robe.

"Holy Jesus, Siobhan. You slept with my baby brother?"

Colm whipped around from the stove and slapped Siobhan on the ass. "There wasn't much sleeping was there, sweet cheeks?" he asked.

Siobhan picked up a dishtowel and flicked it at him.

"For Christ's sake." Cassie threw her hands up in the air.

"We're grown adults, Cassie," Colm said.

"Well, you're grown all right." She rolled her eyes. "You're still a child, but you—what's your excuse?" She pointed at Siobhan.

Cassie heard a cough behind her. "Good morning." Dax fell in line next to Cassie, his hand slipping into place at the curve of her back. She glanced at him briefly. At least he had the decency to dress. It was still one hundred percent obvious he'd spent the night here.

Colm stared at Dax, and Cassie stared at Siobhan. It was a stand-off scene worthy of a Clint Eastwood western. Colm surveyed Dax like any brother might look at his sister's boyfriend. Though, she certainly wouldn't classify Dax as her boyfriend. They may have shared another amazing night together, but she had no illusions to the complications between them. And something told her there was more to it than a simple promise to play boyfriend to a rich girl to keep her daddy happy.

"I can't believe you did this!" She looked at Siobhan. "I

don't mind him, he's a boy who doesn't know how to keep it in his pants, but I expected better from you."

"Oh, for God's sakes. Get down off the cross Cassie, someone else needs the wood." Siobhan took her coffee cup to the dining room table and plopped onto a chair. "And don't yell at me, I've got a wicked hangover." She gave a dismissive wave of her hand before rubbing her temple.

"I'm Dax. Nice to meet you." He held his hand out to Colm.

"Colm." He shook Dax's hand. "St. Cassie's brother."

"Shut up, Colm," Cassie warned.

"Well, this is awkward." Dax looked at Cassie.

"Says the fella who just banged my sister." Colm raised an eyebrow.

Cassie raised a finger. "First, don't speak to Dax like that. Second, you have no right to comment on my love life! After all these years, how could you two go behind my back like this?" The early morning joggers could likely hear her in Central Park.

Neither her best friend nor her brother was the committed type. Sooner, rather than later, they'd realize it and she'd have to pick up the pieces. It was the last thing she could handle right now. Siobhan would do what she always did and disappear without any explanation, which would mean disappearing from Cassie's life. She'd lost so much lately, she couldn't bear to lose Siobhan too.

"It's hardly going behind your back, Cassie. We're right here in your apartment." Colm picked up the coffee carafe and crossed the room to top up Siobhan's cup.

Good thing Cassie didn't have a cup in her hands. She couldn't be responsible for where it landed. She noticed Siobhan stifling a grin.

"I'm glad you're both getting a grand kick out of this."

Cassie put her hands on her hips like an angry mother scolding her children. "Have your fun. You forget I know you both better than you know yourselves." She pointed at Siobhan. "After you realize he's still a boy." She pivoted and pointed at Colm. "And you move on to your next conquest." She pointed at herself. "It'll be me who loses out because neither of you will be able to stand being in the same room with each other. But that's fine! Nobody ever thinks about what Cassie stands to lose because you're all so selfish."

"Cassie, honey." Dax put his arm around her. "Maybe—"

She whipped around to face him. "Don't think for a minute you're going to be the voice of reason here. Since we're talking selfish, what about you?" She tried her hand at a manly American-accented impression. "Oh Cassie, I want you, but it's complicated, Cassie. I need you, Cassie. I'll never break your heart, but I gotta go. My fake girlfriend needs me to take her to a fundraiser."

She was one hundred percent unhinged at this point and for the first time ever, didn't care. For once she was taking a stand. People walked all over her and she was having it no more.

"Vanessa Roberts is your fake girlfriend," Siobhan said. "Hmm, how does that work?"

"Christ, you sure do things different in America," Colm said. "So, this Vanessa is his fake girlfriend and you're his real girlfriend?" He stood behind Siobhan's chair. "Do you divvy up the days on a calendar?" he asked.

Dread filled Cassie as she realized what she'd done. "Shut up, Colm." She focused on Dax and the hurt flooding his eyes.

"You're so quick to point out how wrong it is what I'm doing with Siobhan," Colm continued. "But what about you? What are you doing with a guy who isn't actually with you? That's the pot calling the kettle black, isn't it?"

"Shut up, Colm!"

When did her baby brother become such a voice of reason?

"Dax, I'm—"

"I should go." Dax strode down the hallway to her bedroom with Cassie in tow.

"I'm sorry." She followed him. "I don't know what got into me. I was so angry with them and …" She stopped, watching him from the doorway as he sat on the edge of the bed. He slipped his shoes on and reached for his watch on the bedside table. He stood, lifted his coat from the back of a chair and shrugged it on.

"I didn't mean to out you." She walked over and stood right in front of him.

She wanted nothing more than for him to take her in his arms and explain everything away. To tell her it would all be fine. But he didn't. He stood there, a stony expression clouding his handsome face.

"No, Colm's right." His eyes narrowed. "You deserve better than to be with a guy who isn't actually with you. I'm sorry I can't be that guy."

"Dax, let's talk about this." Her eyes filled and she wrapped her arms around her shoulders, hugging herself. "I thought you felt something for me."

He ran his hands through his hair. "I do. More than you could ever know, but I—" He was silenced by a sharp ring tone. Reaching in his pocket, he palmed his phone and turned it over. As Cassie glanced down a young boy's smiling face flashed across the screen before Dax slid his finger over it and answered the call. He turned his back to Cassie and stepped into her ensuite.

Cassie took refuge in the hallway. She wasn't eavesdropping, but she couldn't help overhearing him either. His tone was serious, almost panicked, and not the level, measured timbre she was accustomed to. She heard references to Mount Sinai and neurology. Something was wrong. Her feelings for Dax were strong, but she practically knew nothing of his life, his family. She knew he was from Boston and had met Zander Roberts there, but that was the extent of her knowledge of one Mr. Dax Carter.

On the flip side, she'd poured her heart out to him the first night they met. She didn't doubt he wanted her physically, but he certainly wasn't ready to let her in. They were doomed before they ever began. Her self-preservation instincts told her to walk. Now. Get off this roller coaster she'd been on since they met. The part of Cassie craving love and happiness told her to re-evaluate. Did she want to walk away from him?

She clenched her fists, never so torn over another human being. She'd dropped Rhys in a heartbeat when he cheated on her. She left him, left Ireland and hadn't looked back. And yet, here she was agonizing over a man she'd only just met. She was negotiating with both sides of her brain—the rational, logical Cassie who said cut loose and run—and the out-of-control Cassie who told herself if he ended the call and let her into his world just a little bit maybe they had a shot.

Her head snapped up, hopeful, as he appeared in the doorway. He met her gaze and looked away. She slumped against the wall—any hopes dashed. He couldn't look her in the eye. Why did she think he was about to walk out of her apartment and her life for good? And given everything she was feeling why didn't she want that?

"I have to go." He didn't meet her eyes.

"Is everything okay?"

A tortured look crossed his face. "No." He shook his head.

"Is it Vanessa? Is she hurt?"

"Vanessa's fine."

"What is it, Dax?"

"I can't talk about this right now." He tried to sidestep her, but she blocked him.

"When can you talk about it?"

He ran his hands through his hair and groaned a fierce sound. Cassie stepped back. "I don't know. Someday. Maybe? No. Look, I'm truly sorry. It's because you do mean something to me that I just can't do this. I can't constantly disappoint you. It was insane to think I could ever have this. Ever have you." He stepped closer, placing his hands on her shoulders. He leaned down and kissed her lightly at first then more urgently, his tongue dipping inside tasting her, as if committing the act to memory.

When he broke away Cassie wobbled slightly. "Why do I get the feeling this is goodbye?" Her breath caught in her throat. Still, she mustered up the courage to ask the question, though she already knew the answer. The backs of his three fingers caressed her cheek and she leaned into his touch.

"I didn't mean to hurt you, Cassie. You're the best thing to come into my life in a long time."

"So, don't. Don't hurt me. And don't let Vanessa do this to you. She must be a terrible person if she doesn't want you to be happy." His blue eyes filled with confusion, hurt, and a myriad of other emotions. A thought struck her. "Unless you've developed feelings for her and you just don't know how to tell me."

"God, no. How could you think that? The times we've been together, I promise I've only been thinking of you. And when I'm not with you, I've been dreaming of you.

My feelings for Vanessa do not extend beyond friendship."

"Fine. Then what aren't you telling me?"

"I'm not choosing Vanessa over you. But I am choosing not to bring you into my complicated world."

"Shouldn't I get to make that choice? I'll admit I'm not thrilled about your pseudo relationship, but there's something you're not telling me. Whatever you're holding on to —whatever you think I can't handle," Cassie said, "is it worth walking away from this?"

He took her hands in his and squeezed them. "Yes." His voice was hoarse. He leaned in and kissed her cheek. "Take care of yourself, Cassie."

The words echoed through her mind like footsteps down a dark, lonely hallway. She heard the quiet click of the door and he was gone. Emptiness shrouded her like a cloak. Emotions she didn't know existed smacked into her as if a chunk of ice the size of a meteor had collided with her heart.

~

Dax was wrought with guilt as he floored the Mercedes away from Cassie's toward Mount Sinai. She deserved to be treated so much better than this. He had to end it. What could he offer her? A lifetime of dropping her to run to Vanessa's side? At some point the Vanessa situation would take care of itself, but there'd always be Adam and the responsibility that went with him. He'd never expected to meet anyone like Cassie, but he couldn't afford to be selfish right now. His life could wait. It had to wait. His first and only priority was Adam. He'd let him down once before and the price had been hefty.

Dax couldn't expect anyone else to take on that

burden. Certainly not a young woman who'd just dodged an almost-marriage and was embarking on a new, carefree life in New York City. When he got to Mount Sinai, he made the familiar trek to neurology and met Vanessa pacing in the hallway.

"Hi." She rushed into his arms.

"Is Stephanie here?" He pulled out of her embrace.

"Yes, she's in with him now."

"What's she saying?"

"His temp is unusually high this morning. They're giving him cold IV fluids and watching his blood pressure carefully."

"Is he awake?"

"No, she gave him a sedative."

"Dammit, I should have been there." His hands rubbed the day-old stubble along his jaw line—a reminder he wasn't his usual clean-shaven self because he hadn't been home yet. He picked up the pacing where Vanessa had left off.

"Dax, you know how this goes. It comes on fast. It didn't happen because you weren't there." She grabbed him by the shoulders. "Hey, listen to me. Stop with the guilt. He's going to be okay. He always is." She smiled and lifted his chin to meet her eyes. "This is the best place for him and Steph is the best."

"I know," he whispered.

All his grief resurfaced and hit him with the impact of a speeding train. Every time Adam experienced an episode of autonomic dysreflexia, Dax relived the night his world changed forever. Somewhere in the back of his mind he wondered if he should contact Marley. A few months ago, he tried the last cell phone number he had and received an out of service message. God only knew where she was and what rock she was living under. He shook the thought from his mind. Adam was better off without her. The elevator doors dinged and the rest of the Roberts family spilled out.

"Why didn't you phone us sooner?" Helen called out, hurrying toward them.

"It was early," Dax said. "We didn't want to wake you." He narrowed his eyes at Vanessa. As rocky as things were between them right now Vanessa wasn't foolish enough to mention he hadn't been at home when Adam was rushed in. She wouldn't want her mother to start asking questions about his whereabouts. She'd also never disrespect him by calling her own folks before him.

Adam had twenty-four-hour care givers, employed through a private company. Vanessa also lived right next door. She had agreed to spend the night with Adam while Dax went out with Zander. Later, he let her know he was spending the night at Cassie's. From the moment he realized he'd developed feelings for Cassie he'd been upfront with Vanessa. Her texts made it clear she didn't like it, but only because she didn't want the situation to get any more out of hand than it was. She'd never say anything to her folks. She wasn't vindictive.

"We didn't want to wake you." Vanessa interjected, placing an arm around Dax, keeping up the pretence.

"What does that matter? We're your family. You know you can always depend on us, day or night." Helen embraced him. "What are they saying?"

"Stephanie is in there with him now, Mom," Vanessa said, as Dax stepped out of Helen's hold.

"That poor little boy." Helen twisted her hands in knots.

"He's going to be okay." It was a statement Dax had made many times and never believed. He noticed the worry lines around Helen's mouth. She was as overbearing as they came, but Dax knew the woman had grown to love

Adam as her own. The Roberts' had given Dax and Adam a home and a family when they needed it most.

"He's so lucky to have Steph watching over him. She is the best," Helen said to no one in particular.

No one would dispute the fact that Dr. Stephanie Reynolds was the best. At forty she was double board-certified in neurology and neurosurgery in pediatrics and sought after by many a medical institution. What wouldn't be shouted from the rooftops was that she was also Vanessa's lover. Only Zander and Dax knew the truth. And now Cassie. His stomach tightened. What a tangled web they'd woven he thought as he looked around at this family. His family in every sense.

Vanessa's gaze met his and Dax narrowed his eyes in a look that said it was way past due to come clean about her and Stephanie's relationship. But they'd had that conversation hundreds of times. He never managed to get her any closer to pulling the trigger. Vanessa's problems were hers to carry alone today. Adam was his only focus. Cassie had been a bright spot in his life and thoughts of her had filled him with hope and a newfound energy. Now, there was nothing but the impending darkness again.

"What can we do for you, Son?" Franklin Roberts clapped a hand on Dax's shoulder. He was taller than Dax and burlier. He was gruff at times and had a well-earned reputation for being a hard-ass, but Dax knew from experience his bark was far worse than his bite.

"You're doing it sir, you've been doing it for four years." Dax wiped at his eyes. "Thank you." Franklin caught him in a hug and Dax knew it was a rare show of emotion for the business mogul.

All heads turned when the double doors opened and Dr. Stephanie Reynolds walked toward them. She came directly to Dax and put an arm around him as the rest of the Roberts clan fanned around them.

"Adam's stable," she said. "We managed to get his body temperature down quickly, avoiding any seizures. He's heavily sedated though, and I'd like to keep him here for a few more days. I'm particularly interested to see if he has another spike in the next twenty-four to forty-eight hours." She squeezed Dax's hand. "Why don't you go in and have a few moments alone with him. After you've seen for yourself, you should all head home and get some rest. I assure you he's going to be out for most of this day."

"Thanks, Stephanie." Dax hugged her. "I don't know what we'd do without you."

"Likewise," she whispered in his ear, winking at him as she drew back. "Come on, let me take you to him."

Adam was out of the woods—this time, but Dax lived with the harsh truth that the next time could be the last time. He let out a long, slow breath and followed Stephanie to his son's hospital room.

CHAPTER 13

THE NEXT FEW WEEKS PASSED IN A HAZE FOR CASSIE. SHE was miserable about the break-up with Dax, if you could call it that. She hadn't heard from him since he left her apartment. A few days after she'd sent him a simple text that said she hoped he was doing okay and that she was thinking about him. It went unanswered. She'd caught a glimpse of him in the boardroom on a few occasions in meetings. Once he looked directly at her. Expressionless. It was time to let him go.

Colm had decided to stick around until Christmas. On her loneliest days, it was a Godsend but he spent most of his time with Siobhan. She knew Siobhan was going home too. She never missed a Christmas in Kilkenny. Cassie was still angry that her best friend and her brother were sleeping together, but she'd given that one up to Jesus. Just because she was destined for a life of unhappiness didn't mean they should be. If they made each other happy for now, who was she to argue? If there was one lesson she'd learned twice in a matter of months—there were no guarantees in this life.

Thankfully, work was busy. Her team had spent a lot of their time on the Museum of Natural History's youth engagement file and she'd met with Victor and his staff regularly. Cassie had gotten the impression on more than one occasion that Victor might be interested in her. He lingered a lot after meetings and found excuses to call her about things Serena could have easily answered for him. At first, she was a little put off by it, the hurt from her brief liaison with Dax still fresh in her mind. The wound in her heart ran as deep as open heart surgery. But little by little, the guy was growing on her—not that she was going to ask him on a date or anything. It was just time to start acknowledging that she couldn't pine away for Dax anymore. It was time to get on with her life.

Victor was handsome in a different way than Dax. Dax was rugged and sophisticated with an air of confidence that wasn't cocky, he just oozed power and strength—classically masculine. Victor was suave and stylish. His mother was Latino and his father was from India. All together the combination worked well. He had deep brown eyes with the longest, thickest lashes she'd ever seen on a man, complemented by a milky chocolate complexion and a strong jawline. His black hair was short in the back, but long enough in the front to have a permanently tousled look. Always impeccably dressed, he was disarming and on many occasions, had drawn Cassie out of her shell by asking questions about Ireland, making comparisons between New York City and Dublin. After their last meeting about the "Night at the Museum" pilot project, which the board of directors thought was brilliant, he hung back and asked to see Cassie in her office.

"What can I do for you?" She closed the door and gestured for him to take a seat.

"I have a question to ask you."

"Shoot." She rounded her desk and lowered herself into her chair.

"Well—" He hesitated. "The Museum's Christmas party is this Friday and I wondered if you might consider coming with me. As my date."

"Oh!" Her face reddened.

"I've embarrassed you."

"No, no, you haven't. Not at all." She touched her cheek. Yup. The littlest bit of attention and she was on fire.

"There's no pressure to say yes. I didn't mean to make you feel uncomfortable."

"And you haven't. That's not it at all."

"Are you seeing someone?" She knew Victor had seen all the same gossip rags as everyone else a few weeks ago, furthering speculation about her and Dax. She looked away, his question lingering in the air. *Don't be stupid, he's a nice guy. Go. Dax is not coming back to you. It's over.*

"No. Free as a bird." She met his eyes, raising an eyebrow. "But." She paused. "I have to admit I'm not cut out for the big black tie affairs."

His face brightened. "Is that your only caveat?"

She laughed. "Pretty much, yeah."

"Well, you're in luck." He leaned in as if telling her a secret. "No black ties. In fact, no ties at all." His smile was sweet. "You know we raise a lot of money for the museum?" She nodded. "Well, we also do a lot of charity work as well. The party kicks off with an ice skating party at Rockefeller Centre around four o'clock, followed by hot chocolate. Any staff who have kids usually bring them along, but we also host around thirty kids from an inner city after school program we run. There's a pizza party after that and when all the kids are gone home, the staff heads to the museum for a little after party, some more sophisticated food, but still no ties." He flashed a smile. "A DJ sets up on the main floor and we have a few drinks and dance the night away."

Cassie listened intently, grinning like a kid. "That sounds amazing. But I have to warn you, I have never put on a pair of ice skates in my life. Though I'd be honoured to be your date." She surprised herself by meaning every word. His smile widened, reaching his eyes, which held a mixture of eagerness and relief. She'd spent so much time stuck at the Dax pity party that she hadn't realized just how much Victor was into her.

"Wonderful. Okay, I'll email you the details." They both stood and she walked him to her office door.

"I guess I'll be off." His ear-splitting grin said he was pleased with himself and Cassie laughed. "See you Friday?"

"Yes." She nodded. "Looking forward to it." The two stared at each for a few seconds. Mounting excitement built as she realized she was looking forward to something. Anything.

As if sensing it, Victor leaned in and kissed her on the cheek. "Until then."

"Until then." She closed the glass door behind him. He turned and raised his hand in a brief wave. She realized she was smiling. It wasn't the full-on excited and lust-filled emotions that Dax evoked in her, but she was happy. She sighed. It was short lived, however. Her smile evaporated as her eyes followed Victor, who turned around and smacked right into Dax, whose rigid stance and cold grey eyes said he'd witnessed their whole exchange. Was that anger she saw on his face? She met his gaze for a split second before she pushed the button near the door frame. The glass walls frosted over, shutting out Dax's image, much like her heart had.

~

It wasn't as if Dax didn't know it was inevitable and honestly, Victor Ramirez was a great guy. But he still wasn't prepared for it. He paced outside her door talking himself out of following Victor to the elevator bank. What could he say? There was no one to blame but himself. He'd been by Cassie's office a couple of times over the last few days hoping to catch a glimpse of her. Maybe say a quick hello and get a general sense of how angry she was.

Things had settled down with Adam again, which was the cycle of his condition and now that Dax's mind had cleared from incessant worrying, he couldn't think about anything but her. He needed to apologize and he wanted to tell her about Adam. He hadn't wanted to scare her off before, but all she'd asked for was honesty. He owed her that.

If he told her the truth maybe he could repair the damage he'd done and earn back some of her trust. At least, he could allay her fears about Vanessa or anyone else in his life of any importance. Besides Adam, there wasn't. But who was he kidding? He had more baggage than the *Titanic*. Adam was a huge responsibility and he was all-consuming. His illness was severe and it was a lot to take on. Then there was the obligation to keep Vanessa's secret. After all—she kept his. He had come to Cassie's office prepared to lay all his cards on the table, but it looked like he was ten minutes too late.

His mind went to sinister places as he trekked back to his office with one thought striking him like a sledgehammer. Was Helen behind this? Victor was good at his job and loyal to Helen and the board, but would he go so far as to date Cassie to keep Helen happy? Slamming his door behind him, Dax paced the floor of his office. Surely, that was too twisted, even for Helen. But he also didn't put anything past the woman. If she felt threatened she wouldn't be above asking for Victor's help.

There had been several hints dropped by both Helen and Franklin this year, who both made it clear they thought it was time Dax and Vanessa took their relationship to the next level. A few days after Adam's hospitalization, Helen had come to his office and had casually asked about Cassie's work performance. It was the first time she'd ever taken an interest in a Crave employee in the two years he'd been CEO. While she had nothing to do with the business end of things, she did hold a PhD in passive-aggressive behaviour. Dax told Vanessa something had to give or they'd soon find themselves the guests of honour at their own wedding, organized by social planner extraordinaire, Helen herself. That had caused a big argument and he'd gone to bed that night thinking this was just like being in a real relationship, but without the makeup sex. And not with the woman he wanted to be with.

As much as Dax longed to paint Helen as the villain here, the cross-examination going on in his mind told him there was one piece of evidence he simply could not ignore. In fact, his expert witness—himself—could shoot his original theory all to hell, if he'd just be honest. It was the look on Victor's face. He was way too pleased with himself to have been executing a favour for Helen. No, Dax knew that look. He'd had that look. For Christ's sake, he still had that look. Victor was into Cassie. And from Dax's observation post outside her door, it looked like the feelings were mutual.

Cassie took out her phone and texted Siobhan.

CK: What does one wear to an ice-skating party?

SO: How the fuck am I supposed to know? I'm from Ireland not Canada. Who's going to an ice skating party anyway?

CK: Me

SO: Can I come? Just to take photos!

CK: So funny. Seriously, I don't know what's appropriate ice skating attire.

SO: Who are you going with?

CK: Why does that matter? Shouldn't whether it's indoors or outdoors matter more? Or what the temperature will be that day?

SO: Always bogged down in the minutia. Those are minor details. It always matters who you're with. Are you trying to impress someone?

CK: Kind of, I guess

SO: Better not be that gobshite Dax. That's from your brother, BTW.

Cassie laughed aloud. Colm—always the protective brother.

CK: You can tell him it isn't. Believe me. I've moved on.

SO: Good to hear. In that case, swing by my apartment tomorrow after work. We'll order take out and I'll kit you out.

CK: OK. See you tomorrow. It's outdoors, if that matters.

SO: It doesn't. Chow babe.

CHAPTER 14

As she made her way down to Rockefeller Centre, Cassie hoped she didn't look too girly. Siobhan had loaned her a pair of black spandex leggings, a cream cashmere turtle neck and a light pink puffy vest, with faux fur around the collar, to go over top. She topped the outfit off with a pale pink knitted boyfriend hat and a pair of grey, knee-length boots. When she checked herself out in the mirror her first thought was she was ready to star in an episode of Barbie's on Ice. Except for her blazing red hair, she was a dead ringer. She spotted Victor, waiting for her at the top of the stairs leading down to the skating rink below.

"Hi," he said, embracing her with a kiss on both cheeks.

"Hi yourself."

"You look—"

"Ridiculous, right?" Cassie laughed. "This is my friend Siobhan's attempt at trendy skating attire, but I'm afraid I had nothing suitable. I'm still just getting settled here in New York." It had been six weeks already, but she'd spent a good portion of that time wallowing over Dax. She'd have been far better off engaging in some retail therapy.

"I was going to say beautiful," Victor said. "Your friend has great taste in clothes, but she also has an amazing canvas to work with." His eyes wandered from her boots up over the rest of her body, before finally meeting her eyes and he smiled appreciatively. Her cheeks heated. If he'd ever taken full stock of her like this before, he'd been more discreet about it.

"Come on." He placed his hand at the small of her back, guiding her down the stairs and Cassie's breath hitched. Her mind flooded with memories of the last man who touched her there. She'd always found that simple act powerful, possessive, almost claiming. She wasn't sure she was ready to let anyone claim her again so soon. She'd gone all-in with Dax and it was the biggest let down of her life. Yes, bigger than Rhys, amazing as that was since she was supposed to be happily married to him by now.

"Let's get you some skates." Victor smiled oblivious to the thoughts running through her head.

One of Victor's colleagues sized Cassie's feet at the makeshift skate shack the museum staff had set up that day to provide skates for kids who didn't have any. Skates in hand they made their way to one of the benches. When Victor was finished with his own he tied hers.

"I feel like one of the children." Cassie laughed as Victor tightened her skates and tied them at the top.

"I'm glad you're not." He pulled her to her feet. Victor was tall already, but he was a giant on skates. Cassie squealed as she wobbled and fell into his arms. "If you were one of the children I couldn't do this—" he pulled her tight and leaned down, brushing his lips lightly against hers.

"Oh," Cassie said when he pulled back.

"Sorry, I couldn't resist." He smiled. "You're very kissable."

"It's ok." She returned his smile. Victor's lips were smooth and he tasted like mint. The kiss was pleasant, but there were no sparks. No flutters in her belly. Not like the kisses she'd shared with Dax. Maybe because he caught her off guard? As she tried to rationalize it she tasted the bitter anger rising within her. Stop this, Cassie. Stop comparing every new experience against Dax. It's not fair to you or Victor. And Victor is the one here right now. He's the one who wants you—Dax does not.

"Ready for the ice?" he asked.

"If I say no, will it matter?"

He laughed. "I got you. Just hold onto my hand."

"You realize if I go down, I'm taking us both?"

"Not going to happen. I'm a pro," Victor said. "Could've been a hockey player."

"How does someone with Mexican and Indian lineage become a professional skater?" She inched forward, taking little steps much like a toddler.

"That's the beauty of the United States of America, Cassie. The land of opportunity," he said, suddenly twirling her around. "Didn't your momma tell you you could be anything you wanted to be?"

She giggled at the sudden movement, knowing she wasn't at all in control. In the interest of not breaking a bone she let Victor control her movements and she followed along. He slowed them down to a stop and stepped in front of her. He grabbed her hands, pulling her along as he skated backward.

"Well my ma died when I was thirteen, but my Nanna still tells me that," she said.

"I'm sorry," he said. "That must have been hard for you."

"It was, yes. For all eight of us."

"Eight? Wow. I thought Latino families were fertile. There's only four of us!"

"Ah, well you may be fertile, Victor, but we're fertile and Catholic," she said, winking at him.

He laughed and twirled her around again. Hand in hand, they skated around the crowded ice, laughing and sharing family stories. After half an hour, she mastered a lap on her own. Cassie had gotten the hang of it rather quickly, but believed Victor ignored her progress so he could keep holding her hand. She hadn't minded one bit. She sat on a bench, waiting for him to return with a cup of hot chocolate while she surveyed the ice. The surface was packed full of adults and kids of varying ages laughing, stumbling, and enjoying the afternoon.

Cassie loved children. Nanna Kit used to joke that her biological clock had been ticking since she was ten. She couldn't think of a time when she hadn't looked forward to being a mom. A pang of sadness settled inside. She had her heart set on getting pregnant immediately after she and Rhys got married, though he'd always seemed lukewarm to the idea. In the days after their breakup, the loss of impending motherhood was the most upsetting. Of course, that wasn't reason enough to marry Rhys, but she still ached from carrying around the thought of possibly being pregnant by now.

Something caught her eye at the other end of the ice. A man spinning around a young boy in a wheelchair. The squeals of delight coming from the boy were heartwarming. The man laughed too and after slowing down the chair he crouched in front of the boy, who threw his arms around the man, whom she assumed was the boy's father. Her eyes filled with tears. The way the two hugged, the reciprocal love, it was almost too much to watch. A woman skated up to them and the boy's face lit up. He gave her a high five and a hug almost as big as the one he'd given his father. The bond with the father was clearly superior. Now, that was devotion. Raising a child with a disability couldn't be a cake walk for either of them.

"That right there is the most amazing and selfless man you will ever meet."

Cassie jumped, startled by the visitor who sat next to her on the bench.

"But I'm guessing you already know this."

"Mrs. Roberts," Cassie said. She'd have jumped to her feet in surprise, but the skates prevented that from being an option. "Who and what are we talking about?"

"Okay, let's play it your way," Helen said. "The only reason I haven't insisted on your termination is because you're smart and you may actually be on to something with your plans for the museum. And because of Victor. He's head over heels for you, which couldn't have worked out any better than if I had thought of it myself. But I will get rid of you if I have to."

"My termination? I'm sorry, Mrs. Roberts, but have I done something to offend you?" The woman was measured, but there was no disputing the hard line to her tone. Obviously, this had something to do with Dax. Clearly, she hadn't gotten the memo that whatever brief fling they'd had was well and truly over. Where the hell was Victor? He needed to get his ass back here now.

"Don't get me wrong, I can see the appeal. Young, pretty, smart, and that accent is strangely charming," Mrs. Roberts continued.

Cassie decided Victor or no Victor she was getting out of this Twilight Zone experience. But first, she had to get these skates off. She pulled at the laces.

"I know you've turned his head, but so what? They all

stray occasionally." She shrugged. "It happens. My Franklin has done so a time or two. The main thing is the good ones have a moral compass and they will always come back home." She pointed down the ice. "And that one there, well, he'll never leave my daughter. He'll never leave our family."

Cassie looked up as she pulled off one skate. She followed the woman's pointing finger in the direction of the couple and the boy in the wheelchair. The trio were a lot closer now. The little boy was waving at her. No. He couldn't be waving at *her*. She didn't know him. Her eyes moved up to the man pushing his chair. When she met Dax's eyes, she froze. She looked from the boy to Dax and back again. Same black hair, same cool, blue eyes.

Dear God. Blood rushed to her head.

"Hello, darling," Helen called out and the little boy waved harder, a big smile widening on his face. The woman returned the wave and stood, but before she ventured onto the ice she turned back to Cassie. "How could you live with yourself if you broke up his family? That boy is his world. Surely, you have enough decency to realize a quick romp cannot replace family. And this boy needs his mother and his father." Helen opened the side door of the outdoor rink and stepped on, skating towards them.

Cassie couldn't think. Christ, she'd only managed to get one skate off yet. She lowered her head and tried to untie the other lace, but her hands trembled so much all she did was grab unsuccessfully at the laces. Picking up the stubborn skate to sit it on her leg, it slipped and sliced clear across the back of her left hand, along her wrist. Blood spurted, but she felt no pain. She felt nothing. Somewhere in her head a rattling sound took over. It was mild at first, but it got louder until all she could hear was a clacking. *Can anyone stop that noise?*

She was cold. As if she'd done the polar dip, in the Hudson River, naked. *Please somebody, stop that noise.* She heard her name in the distance but ignored it. She had to get out of there. Now. *Stop that fucking noise!* She finally pulled the laces free and tore the skate off, tossing it under the bench.

"Cassie!"

Where were her boots?

"Cassie!"

Dax's voice clouded her mind. Never mind the boots. She jumped off the bench and ran through the crowd, frantic to reach the stairs.

"Cassie, please wait!"

She took the stairs two at a time and kept running trying to get out of Rockefeller Plaza. When she hit West 49th she almost ran into the street. Blood ran from her hand, but she didn't stop. She tore the pink hat from the top of her head and stuffed her hand inside not so much to stop the blood, but more to hide her wound so a taxi driver wouldn't hesitate to pick her up. She hailed a taxi, jumped in the backseat and gave the driver Siobhan's address. She wasn't thinking straight, but she knew she shouldn't be alone right now. As the taxi pulled away from the curb, she jumped when a fist pounded on its door. The taxi jammed on the brakes and she looked up into Dax's pleading face.

"Please, Cassie, don't go like this. Let me explain!" She registered his frantic voice through the window. She stared up at the face of this man, whom she was sure a few weeks ago she was falling in love with, and couldn't hold the tears back any longer. Tears flooded her cheeks as she stared at him through the glass.

"Hey lady, am I staying or am I going?" the driver asked.

"What?" Cassie asked, tearing away from Dax's face long enough to answer him.

"The dude banging on my taxi cab, he's asking you to stay. Are you staying or going?"

She looked back at Dax, who's own face was moist as he pleaded with her to get out of the car. She wanted nothing more than to step outside and into his arms, but Helen's words echoed in her mind. She placed her good hand against the window flat against Dax's hand for a brief second before turning her body away from the window.

"Drive."

This time the driver pulled into traffic, but she could still hear Dax calling to her, his voice more and more frantic. She pulled her cold, bootless feet under her in the back of the cab. Her phone rang. She pulled it from her coat pocket. Dax. She silenced it. It lit up every ten seconds as he continued to call and text, but she couldn't bear to look at any of them. She turned the phone off. Traffic was bad and the car inched forward. Somewhere between 53rd and 57th Street the noise in Cassie's head finally stopped. Oddly enough, her teeth had also stopped chattering. Her vision tunnelled and she leaned back in the seat giving way to a cold blanket of darkness.

CHAPTER 15

DAX WANTED TO HAUL VICTOR RAMIREZ ONTO THE ICE AT Rockefeller Centre and beat the ever-living daylights out of him for several reasons. One—for asking Cassie out in the first place. Two—for bringing her to the Christmas party where she'd been forced to find out things about Dax's life he should have had the guts to tell her himself. And three —letting her fall prey to Helen Roberts. But that wouldn't solve anything. Dax only had himself to blame for this. If only he'd told her the truth.

When he realized who Helen was keeping company with on the bench, fear shot through him like a lightning bolt. The closer he got to Cassie, it wasn't only the shock on her face that shattered him, but the look of betrayal—not for lies—but for truths untold. Which, from her view-point, would seem as bad. It was as bad. She fled before he could get off the ice. He wasn't sure how, but she'd hurt herself in the process, making her easy to find on the street. All he had to do was follow the trail of blood.

She looked so small and fragile in the back of the taxi, so hurt, and when she looked away from him and told the driver to go, he died a little inside. He called and texted her, but she didn't answer. Could he blame her? Well, he was damn well taking matters into his own hands now. If she wouldn't use technology to talk to him he'd leave her no choice but to speak to him in person.

He couldn't let things get any more out of hand. Seeing him with Vanessa wouldn't have elicited that reaction alone. But she saw Adam and put it together. And there was no doubt whatever she hadn't pieced together, Helen had filled in. But how much of it was truth versus Helen's wishful thinking? When the taxi pulled up to her building, Dax tossed a fifty-dollar bill in the front seat and headed to the doors.

"Good evening. Mr. Carter, right?" Dax recognized the friendly doorman, standing right outside.

"Oh, hey there Charlie. Any chance you can let me up to Miss Kennedy's apartment?"

"Well, I can't do that without asking her first, as you know, but you're out of luck anyway because she's not here."

"Oh?"

"She left hours ago. Said she had a skating date or some such thing. Must be going well." He eyed Dax carefully. "I guess it wasn't with you."

"Sadly, no."

"Well, I'll be sure to let her know you stopped by." Charlie gave him a sympathetic smile.

"Thanks, Charlie." He turned and went back down the steps.

"Want me to get you a cab, Mr. Carter?" Charlie called out.

"No, thanks," Dax called over his shoulder. "I could do with the walk."

A few blocks from Cassie's apartment building, Dax

stepped inside a cafe. He glanced at his phone. Nearly nine. He ordered a coffee and took a seat at a corner table, considering his options. When his phone rang, he held a glimmer of hope that it was her. That hope didn't last long.

"Zander, man, it's not a good time," Dax said.

"Yeah, well, you're going to want to hear this," his friend said.

"What's up?"

"I just hung up from Siobhan O'Mara—you know, the hot blonde from Vegas? Cassie's friend?

"Yeah, I know who she is. Get to the point."

"It's Cassie."

His heart pounded. "What about her?" He couldn't erase the image of her running through Rockefeller Plaza with no shoes, holding her injured hand. He'd never forget her running away from him. The guilt was immeasurable.

"She's at Mount Sinai. She cut her wrist on a skate."

"I knew she did something because I followed the blood trail all the way to 49th Street, but I never got close enough to her to look at it." She wouldn't *let* him get close enough. He closed his eyes and shook his head.

"It's pretty serious, Dax. She lost a lot of blood and passed out in the back of a taxi in front of Siobhan's apartment. They called an ambulance and got her in as quick as they could. Apparently, the skate cut through a major vein and they're worried about the possibility of nerve damage. She's being prepped for surgery."

"Fuck." Dax ran a hand through his hair. "This is all my fault."

"How do you figure?"

"I never told her about Adam. She found out about him at the museum's party. She saw me and your sister and Adam together and by the time I realized what was happening, Helen was with her. No doubt she worked her over a bit. Cassie cut her hand trying to get the skates off to get out of there."

"Jesus. I should've known Helen had something to do with this. A two-minute conversation with that woman can be like boxing with your hands tied behind your back in a ring with Mike Tyson."

"I don't know what she said to her, but I can only assume how the 'Dax's life according to Helen speech' made her feel."

"I'm sorry, man," Zander said.

"Listen, I'm going to head over to the hospital. I'm sure she's not going to want to see me, but it doesn't matter. I need to know she's okay."

"Yeah, okay. Keep me posted."

"I will. And thanks for calling me."

Dax hung up the phone and placed his head in his hands, his mind going in ten directions. His first call would be Gina Lombardi at Crave to put Cassie on an extended medical leave with full benefits, until she could return to work. Cassie didn't need to know there weren't any real provisions for this under her current contract. If Gina valued her job she wouldn't be the one to spill it either. If Cassie caught wind of the fact that Dax was behind this she'd undoubtedly turn it down. She'd suffered enough. If she had no income she'd likely return to Ireland and he didn't want to risk that either. He'd have to choose his next act carefully so he didn't frighten her away.

Right now, he could only worry about what he could control and that was making sure she was fully taken care of. If he encountered any roadblocks, he'd go directly to Franklin to make sure the man understood everything. And everything included Vanessa. He was done with this bullshit. But before that he had a more important phone call to make. He opened his contact list and pressed the call button.

Stephanie answered on the first ring. "Is it Adam?"

There was a reason he adored Stephanie. Her commitment to Adam was second to none. "No Adam is fine, but I need a favour."

~

An incessant beeping invaded her ears and when it wasn't that, it was people whispering around her. She finally opened her eyes to see the source of all the activity.

"Jesus Christ, Cassie. You had us worried to death." Colm leaned over and kissed her cheek. He took out his phone, his two thumbs flying furiously across the screen.

She sat up and looked around at the white walls, the equipment and the mint-green gown she wore. "I'm in the hospital?" She let her head fall back against the pillow when the dizziness set in.

"Yes." Siobhan stood on her other side. "You passed out in the back of a taxi, outside my brownstone. We were on our way out. The taxi driver found you covered in blood and called an ambulance."

"I cut my hand." She looked down at her left hand, which was bandaged, and the image of the skate slicing below her wrist rushed back. She tried to move it around, but it was too tender.

Siobhan rubbed her arm. "Cass, honey, it was a little more than a cut on the hand. There was also the two pints of blood you lost. You've been in and out for two days."

"What!" She was hoarse. She struggled to sit up again, hardly believing Siobhan, but the fogginess in her head pushed her back down. "That's not possible."

"What do you remember?" Colm asked.

"I—" Dax and his little boy with Vanessa, Helen Roberts telling her she was no more than a floozy, it all came flooding back. Two images stood out in her mind. The one of Dax's little boy throwing his arms around his father and the final image of Dax's hand on the taxi's window as he pleaded with her to get out and talk to him. The images clicked through her mind as if she were swiping through photos on her phone. "Not much," she lied, looking back and forth between Siobhan and Colm. She couldn't find the words to explain.

"I told the doctor it was your first time ice skating," Siobhan said. "She said, it was a pretty clean slice. Apparently, you're supposed to keep the blades on the ice." She grinned.

"I don't understand why they kept me for that. Couldn't they have stitched me up and sent me on my way?"

"Oh, you're stitched up all right." Colm shivered, having never been one for blood and cuts.

"After they did an emergency repair on your ulnar vein and grafted your arm," Siobhan said. Cassie's eyes widened. "And Colm had to sign for you to have a blood transfusion. He had to prove it wasn't against your religion or some strange thing. I told them we're Catholic—we can have blood transfusions, we just can't have any fun."

Cassie tried to laugh at Siobhan's joke, but it was a lot to take in.

"It's going to take a while to heal, but there's no nerve damage," Siobhan said.

"Nerve damage? Are they sure?" Cassie's voice croaked. She pointed to a pitcher of water on the side table. Siobhan poured some into a cup and held the straw to Cassie's lips.

"Oh, they're sure. There was some fancy neurosurgeon

here when they did your surgery. Courtesy of lover boy." Colm snorted.

Siobhan and Cassie exchanged looks.

"Dax was here?" she asked.

Siobhan nodded. "He's been here every day to check on you, but Colm won't let him in the room." Cassie continued to look back and forth between her brother and her best friend.

"And while we're on the topic of nearly bleeding to death, you owe me a new hat, pants, shirt and vest. And by the way, where the fuck are my boots?"

Cassie laid back and closed her eyes. Her head swam with images. Between the hurt and the drugs, she couldn't process all the information. Sure, Dax had come to the hospital to check on her and he'd arranged for a neurologist, but those actions were driven by guilt not love. She couldn't think about him right now. The haze came and shrouded her like a warm blanket. She gave into it and slipped into the peaceful quiet.

~

"Okay, spill it," Siobhan said later that afternoon after she sent Colm downstairs for coffee. "What the hell happened?"

Cassie sighed. "Oh Shi, things are such a mess." She sat up with a start. "Oh God. Victor. My skating date. He's got to be wondering what happened. I just disappeared."

"I spoke to him. He called your phone a few times. And he was here yesterday. Brought those." Siobhan pointed to a bright bouquet of flowers on a table across the room. "Perhaps you can try something less life-threatening for your second date." She tousled Cassie's hair.

"Oh, I doubt there'll be a second date. I'm sure he's one of a long line of people who aren't speaking to me."

"Why babe? What have you done to piss everybody off?"

"Fell in love with the wrong man." Cassie offered a smile, but failed miserably. "Have you spoken to Dax?"

"We may have had a small chat. See those over there?" Siobhan pointed to a window ledge on the opposite side of the room. Cassie followed her friend's finger, her eyes wide. It was chocked full of every size and type of flower available in the New York area. "They're from Dax."

"How did he know I was here?"

"I called Zander. I needed Gina's number to report your absence and condition to Crave, once we realized the seriousness of the situation. I think it's safe to say news spread to the CEO pretty fast."

"Christ. Does everyone know Helen Roberts reduced me to a petrified mess and I inadvertently sliced my wrist trying to get away from her?"

"I didn't know that's what happened." Siobhan rubbed Cassie's hand. Concern clouded her features. "Though Dax suspected she'd worked you over well, judging by the look of shock on your face when he got close enough to see you. Mrs. Roberts said you two exchanged a few pleasantries and you went on your way."

"Send her the bill for your boots. She's why I left without them."

"Oh, Cassie I don't care about the boots. Well, I do—" Siobhan paused and shook her head. "But I care more about you. What did she say to you?"

"It really doesn't matter what she said. Dax has a son. In a wheelchair. He's beautiful." She smiled. "He's the spit of Dax." Her smile faded. "He and Vanessa and the child are a family in every sense. I saw them together. Helen tied it all up in a neat little bow for me. Her delivery was cruel, but I guess she did me a favour, in a way. I've been pining over a man who isn't mine for weeks now. And now I'm certain he can never be mine. Whatever is or isn't between him and Vanessa, they are a family. I can't be responsible for busting that up."

"That's fair. But do you think you should hear him out?"

What's this? Intelligent, thoughtful insight from the no-strings-attached love expert.

"What's there to hear out? He has a child. I respect that, but he clearly didn't think it was worth mentioning. And he certainly didn't think we should meet." She shook her head. "No, I need to make a clean break, Shi. He's hurt me enough. I've *let* him hurt me enough."

Tiredness overtook her and she turned on her side, arranging her throbbing arm on a pillow. She pushed the button to trigger the morphine drip. Doctors sure weren't anything to write home about, were they? How could they fix the cut on her hand, but couldn't do anything about her shattered heart?

CHAPTER 16

"THAT WAS EASY." CASSIE HUNG UP THE PHONE AS COLM refilled her coffee cup and laid a plate of toast and scrambled eggs in front of her.

"Here, eat this. It's no full Irish, mind you, but I'll fix that when we get home," he said.

"So, what did Gina say?" Siobhan asked.

"Apparently, the contract I signed with Crave includes extended medical leave and there's no reduction in salary. Isn't that amazing?" Siobhan and Colm exchanged a quick look.

"It's great news, especially since I used your credit card last night to book our flights home," Colm said.

"Cheeky." Cassie swatted his arm with her good hand.

Siobhan and Colm had convinced her no matter what the outcome with human resources, going home for a few weeks while she recovered would be good for her. At first, she wasn't in love with the idea but it had grown on her. She didn't want her family to think she'd failed in New York or she'd fled when the first obstacle appeared.

Siobhan had convinced her it wouldn't be unusual to go home for Christmas.

The fact that she'd had an unfortunate accident was beside the point, but it only meant she could stay a little longer while her hand fully recovered. The neurologist, who had done her surgery and visited her daily as part of her follow-up, said it would take at least two months before it healed and she'd need some physical therapy to get her muscle strength back. A little Kennedy family TLC was just what the doctor ordered.

"When are we leaving?" Cassie asked.

"Tomorrow night," Colm said. "We'll head over to your place and I'll get you packed up. Siobhan can meet us there and we'll get a taxi from there to the airport."

"You'll get me packed up? Well, there's a first for everything." Cassie curled her feet underneath her and sipped her coffee.

"Yeah, don't get used to it." Colm looked perfectly at home as he headed into Siobhan's kitchen and Cassie shot her friend a look.

"That's an interesting sight." Cassie nodded toward the kitchen. "My brother making himself at home in your apartment and your kitchen and you're not climbing the walls yet? What's it been? Six weeks?"

Siobhan shrugged, looking at her phone. "Yeah, maybe, but who's counting?" She was engrossed in some emails and barely registered Cassie's comment.

"I am. That's the equivalent of a fifty-year marriage for you two."

"Always so dramatic." Siobhan waved her away, engrossed in her phone.

The fact that Siobhan wasn't counting was the issue. It was out of character. Cassie opened her mouth to counter when Siobhan cut her off without looking up from her phone.

"So, are you going to call Dax before you leave to say goodbye, have a Merry Christmas or kiss my arse?"

"Hadn't planned on it, no." Cassie picked up her own phone, unable to master the blasé look Siobhan had perfected. It was awkward to use a smart phone one-handed. She cursed.

"Well, focus on your own glass house, Cassie Kennedy, and stay the hell out of mine."

~

Dax pulled up in front of Cassie's building. He'd been as patient as possible, but his patience had officially run out. It was Christmas Eve. He had to see her. Cassie's brother had refused to let him anywhere near her while she was in the hospital so he called Stephanie for daily reports on her progress. He didn't trust many people but he trusted Stephanie Reynolds. Hell, he trusted her with Adam's life, so he knew the woman was the best around. By the fourth day, when he knew she was fully awake and functioning, but hadn't asked for him—he took the hint.

He also had it out with Helen. He'd been held hostage by this situation long enough. It should have never gotten this far. He'd been happy to help Vanessa as much as he had. It was the least he could do after all the Roberts family had done for him. They had accepted he and Adam, while helping to fix his train wreck of a life. It wasn't something easily forgotten.

But he couldn't live his life like this anymore. Not since Cassie blew into his life like a Texas hurricane and flattened everything around him. Apart from Adam, who'd always come first, she'd become the only thing he thought about anymore. He'd royally fucked up where she was concerned, but he'd finally made the mental break with the Roberts family. He didn't out Vanessa, he couldn't. The mental stress was something he understood all too well and wouldn't be responsible for, but he'd forced her hand into one of two choices: tell her folks they had broken up, and it was mutual, or come clean about Stephanie and her double life.

It was her choice, but he hoped she chose the latter because it was too hard to keep secrets. How well he knew. He had a big one of his own. Love often forces people to make difficult decisions. And this was hers. How she handled it was her own business, but it was time for Dax to move on. With Cassie, if she'd still have him.

He had rehearsed his speech the whole way to her place and was confident about the outcome. He knew she had strong feelings for him. Their physical connection was intense, but the emotional side was there too and it was the key to a relationship. He jumped out of the taxi with a spring in his step and bounded up the stairs. He glanced at his watch. It was just before eight. She should be resting at home. His only complication was Colm, who wouldn't want to let him in, but he had a speech prepared for him too. He rang the buzzer at the main door and Charlie appeared.

"Evening, Mr. Carter."

"Good evening, Charlie. Can you ring up to Miss Kennedy's apartment for me?"

"I'm sorry but Miss Kennedy is gone, sir."

"Gone?" A sinking feeling hit Dax square in the stomach.

"Miss Kennedy and her brother and their friend, Siobhan. They're gone home for Christmas. I flagged them a taxi to JFK last night. Excited bunch if I've ever seen one."

"To Ireland?"

"Yes, sir." Charlie chuckled. "They were down here in the foyer talking over each other a mile a minute. And that accent. Lord, when the three of them got going I couldn't understand one word."

"Christ, Charlie, don't you ever give any good news?"

The man's smile faded. "Not my problem you've got terrible timing, Mr. Carter."

"You're right. I'm sorry." Dax turned to leave.

"Will you take some advice from an old man?"

"I'd take advice from a cat right now if I thought it could help me get through to Cassie."

"All right, well listen up good. Some women come into our lives for a short while and before you know it, they're gone again. I call them the practicing kind. And I'm not talking about the sex. We date them, your generation may live together a short while and suddenly the zing is gone. There's nothing wrong with these ladies, but they don't suit our tastes. We can't envision a lifetime with them, you follow me, Mr. Carter?"

"I do, yes."

"Good. You see Miss Kennedy, she ain't the practicing kind. She's the keeping kind. The marrying kind. She's the one you want to wake up to every morning. She's the one you want to raise your kids with. Laugh together, cry together and move into the old age home together. She's the one you want to wake up next to in forty years. You still following me, young man?"

"Yes, sir. Sound wisdom. Your wife is a lucky woman."

"I try, Mr. Carter. I try. You can't ever stop trying."

"How am I going to get her back?"

"Oh well, see that's up to you. My guess is you start by buying a plane ticket to Ireland."

Dax laughed. "Well, that's obvious. I was hoping for

something more profound since you seem to have all the answers."

"I think that's the extent of my wisdom meter tonight, son."

"Thanks, Charlie."

"No sweat." Charlie tipped his hat and opened the door wide as Dax stepped outside and headed down the stairs. "Have a good evening, now."

Dax hadn't had a good evening since he walked out of Cassie's apartment more than a month ago.

"You too, Charlie."

"Oh and Mr. Carter?"

"Yeah?"

"Meow." The older man's eyes twinkled and Dax laughed.

Never underestimate the intuitive skills of a New York City doorman. Like bartenders, they'd seen enough human interaction to fill a book.

~

The last time Cassie took a transatlantic flight she was filled with uncertainty and dread. She'd been seriously damaged over the end of her relationship with Rhys and plagued with trepidation over the start of a new life in New York City. It was only seven weeks ago, but it seemed like a lifetime had come and gone. Rhys was a distant memory. If he wanted Amy O'Halleran, Cassie was happy for them. Truly. She could eagerly go to the wedding, sit in the front row and catch the bouquet afterwards, all with a smile on her face.

That's also how she knew she was in love with Dax.

It should have been impossible. She'd hardly adjusted to the time change in New York and already Dax had spun her heart round and reeled it in like a fly in a spider web. She could try to deny it and chastise herself for being impetuous. She'd been doing it for weeks. She'd told herself repeatedly there was no way to fall in love in a matter of weeks, but the reality stared her in the face. Her heart knew it. Her head knew it. She also knew it was a dead end.

It'd be so much easier if she could hate him. Chalk the whole thing up to a bad experience and write him off for being a grade A asshole. But that wasn't true. In fact, it was the farthest thing from truth. How could she be angry with a man who chose his son over a woman? Once the fog cleared, she realized it might just be what she loved most about him. When that little boy threw his arms around Dax's shoulders, her heart nearly exploded as she witnessed the purest expression of love. The love of a child. The love of *his* child. A child he never even told her he had. With Vanessa Roberts. Why couldn't he just have told her about his life? About his child.

It all made so much more sense now—the territorial nature of the Roberts's hold over Dax. But how did that work? Dax said he'd never been with Vanessa like that, so it must have been an in vitro pregnancy. And what about Vanessa's partner? What must she think of it all? Vanessa had gone to great lengths to make her parents believe she was in a healthy heterosexual relationship with Dax. That alone was mind-boggling. But a child? What a commitment. It also meant a lifelong bond with the Roberts family. She'd told herself repeatedly she'd dodged a bullet and she should be happy about that.

Her head ran through the same hamster wheel routine it always did when she tried to rationalize the situation. It was too much for her to think about. No matter how much she wanted Dax, Cassie would not break up a family. No way. Her challenge, while she was home in Kilkenny over Christmas, was to talk her heart and her head onto the same page. There was no going back there. The first order of business when she got back to New York was talking Siobhan into helping her find a new job. She didn't want to think about leaving Serena and Josh and the rest of the team, but staying at Crave was a mistake. There was Dax. Worse still, there was the barracuda. She wouldn't give that woman the satisfaction of firing her.

As the plane broke through the clouds upon its descent into Dublin, Cassie glanced out the window. Ireland claimed to be the home of over forty shades of green and as she studied the green fields that framed out the small island, she marvelled at the accuracy of the claim. She loved Ireland to her core, but already she missed the hustle and bustle of the big city. While no one was more surprised than Cassie to find her taste for the bright city lights of New York resonated more with her than she thought, it didn't change how anxious she was to step through the doors of Kennedy's Pub and into her family's welcoming arms. Thoughts of running into Rhys would've worried the old Cassie, but not this Cassie Kennedy. No, Cassie 2.0 was a new model. A confident, determined woman who'd had a few knocks and learned some hard lessons.

But she was a lot wiser now.

CHAPTER 17

"YOU THINK THIS IS GOING TO WORK?" VANESSA ASKED AS Dax stepped out of the small bedroom located at the back of the Roberts family jet.

"What have I got to lose?" He'd tucked Adam into the bed and strapped him in so his little body wouldn't shift with turbulence. He sat down in one of the leather chairs across from Vanessa.

"That's why we're here." Stephanie snapped the door back into place on the fully-stocked credenza that served as a bar, located on the left-hand side of Franklin's Lear jet. She handed Dax a glass of scotch. "Here's some Dutch courage. Knock it back." She smiled. "Doctor's orders." She took her seat opposite Dax and next to Vanessa. She slid her hand into Vanessa's and lifted it to her lips in an affectionate gesture. "I mean, what could go wrong?"

"Well, I'll admit flying three thousand miles to confess your undying love to a woman, with your fake girlfriend, her lesbian lover and your eight-year old son in tow, is a little unconventional, but when you put it that way, what can go wrong?" Vanessa sipped on a glass of red wine.

"I'm sorry I dragged you across the Atlantic, but I need to show her she's important to me and I can't leave Adam behind, especially during Christmas, so this is the only viable way."

"Hey, no complaints here. I needed some time away from the family nest, believe me. The only way to survive the bomb I dropped on Franklin and Helen on Christmas Day was by getting out of dodge for a little while. Let the nuclear dust settle a bit, you know?" Vanessa shot Stephanie a side-long glance and sipped her wine again.

"I'm sorry you went through that alone," Stephanie said. "I should have been there with you."

"No, it's fine. It was long overdue and I should have had the courage to do it years ago. It took Dax falling in love with the woman of his dreams to make me see how important it is to live your life and not be afraid to fight for the one you love." Vanessa squeezed Stephanie's hand.

"I'm proud of you, Van," Dax said.

"Well, I wouldn't have done it without you, so thank you."

"Yes, thank you Dax. Always there when we need you most." Stephanie raised her glass. "I'd do anything for that little boy in there, you know that."

"And how lucky are we that you have." He raised his glass in return.

They were a close-knit bunch for a host of unorthodox reasons. Not only was it abnormal, but also unfathomable to most people. How had he expected Cassie to react to it all? He couldn't let her slip away from his life without trying to explain it to her. The cockpit door opened and Zander popped out. He tossed his hat on a leather bench seat along the right side of the plane.

"What does a pilot have to do to get a drink around here?" he asked.

"What the hell?" Dax sat straight up in his seat, staring at his best friend. "What are you doing here?"

"I'm wounded you didn't think to bring me on your Irish getaway."

"Listen, man, I'm sorry. It all happened so fast, I—"

"Never mind that, I'm only kidding." Zander poured a scotch and downed it.

"Hang on," said Stephanie. "I hate to be the voice of reason, but if you're out here, who's flying the plane?" She walked over and snatched the glass out of Zander's hand.

Vanessa laughed. "The pilot is flying the plane. He filed the flight plan and I shook his hand when we got here. Don't worry, Steph."

"Ah, Sis, I had her good. Why'd you have to ruin it?" Zander laughed.

"Thank God." Stephanie flopped in her chair, reaching for her glass.

"And while we're on the topic of ruining things. Dax, I have sympathy for. But Christ woman, how could you have not warned me that you came clean to Franklin and Helen? Like, seriously, what have I done to you to warrant that kind of punishment? Letting me walk into a shit-storm of epic proportions without any warning? That's harsh, girl. We're blood. Merry Christmas to you."

"Sorry." Vanessa cringed. "It's like Dax said. It all happened so fast. As did the hatching of this plan. How did you find out where we were?"

"I was at the airfield when the fax came in—hoping to plan a little getaway to Cabo. When I saw the manifest, it didn't take me long to realize what he was doing." He shot a glance at Dax. "The lovesick fool. When I arrived home, I discovered the remnants of your confession. Obviously, I packed a bag and got the hell out of dodge."

"How bad is it?" Vanessa wrinkled her nose.

"Pretty bad. Helen is looking for rehabilitation centres online and Franklin was three quarters into a bottle of Jack."

"She's trying to put him in rehab?" Dax asked.

"God no, the rehab is for Van. She thought Franklin's response was perfectly normal."

The four of them laughed as Zander poured another scotch and took a seat next to Dax. "So, what's the plan?" Zander asked.

"Still unfolding," Dax said.

"We're his back-up, in case things don't go well." Vanessa pointed back and forth between her and Stephanie.

"Man, you need some serious tips on wooing women if you're hedging your bets on two lesbians. Good thing I'm a stowaway. I might save your love life yet." Zander winked and raised his glass. "Merry Christmas."

"I can't say as I'm happy you hurt yourself." Cassie's father, Brendan, looked down at her arm. "But I'm sure happy it brought you home to us for Christmas." He wrapped his arms around her.

"Da, I've only been gone a few weeks. Watch the arm." Cassie winced and lifted it up and out of his strong embrace.

"Feels more like a year," he said.

"What did I tell you was going to happen to you over there?" Nanna Kit asked.

"Nanna, I wasn't mugged and left for dead in an ally. It was a skating accident." Cassie left it at that. It was easier not to get into details.

"Skating?" The pitch of Nanna's voice matched her raised eyebrows.

"Yes, you know, where you put blades on your feet and skate around a rink."

"What is that, some bizarre American mating ritual?"

Cassie laughed. "No, it's a sport, actually, but people also do it for enjoyment."

"Sounds agonizing."

"It's not." It had been a lot of fun, at least until the end. Listening to Helen Roberts could be classified as agonizing, and the rest was kind of a blur.

Nanna pulled her in close again. "This doesn't have anything to do with Rhys, does it?" She whispered in Cassie's ear.

"What? No! Not a chance. No. Rhys is history. Ancient history. He and Amy are a good match. I hope they find happiness together."

"I hope she gives him the clap," Nanna said. "You're too forgiving."

Cassie shrugged. "Being away has given me clarity on the whole affair."

"Is that so?" Nanna narrowed her eyes at Cassie. "And does this *being away* happen to have a last name?"

"No, of course not." Cassie's face reddened. Jesus Christ, was she an open book? "Why'd you say that?" It was pointless. She'd never had been a good liar. Nanna had always seen right through her. "I'm not into holding grudges. What's the point?"

"The point is you're Irish. Holding grudges is genetic. So, if you're not, there's a reason. I'd like to know the reason's name. Stop lying to your grandmother."

"I'm not lying, Nanna. I'm choosing not to get into it. There's a big difference."

"Not to me there isn't."

"It doesn't matter anyway. It was nothing." Nanna believed everything happened for a reason. Cassie was never sure she bought into all that crap, but maybe that was the reason Dax had come into her life. To help her put the break up with Rhys into perspective. Maybe it was never supposed to be anything other than that.

"I wondered how long it would be before you started spilling your guts about lover boy." Colm stepped behind the bar and pulled himself a pint of Guinness.

"Bingo." Nanna grinned.

"Colm, it's only half ten in the morning, can't you at least wait until we open?" Their father bellowed from the cold room off the bar.

"How'd you know it was me?"

"Because your sister is far too sensible to get into the drink before noon."

"That's our Cassie. The sensible one," Colm muttered. "She's seeing a man who has a child he never told her about. Did I mention the man is her boss? The child is from a fake relationship he has with the daughter of the man who owns the company. The woman is some kind of vegetarian lesbian, who dates him in name only to keep her parents off her back. And Cassie's the sensible one?" Colm picked up the Guinness and downed it.

"Can someone tell me what a vegetarian is?" asked old Mr. Kelly from next door, who had assumed his regular post in the corner. Everyone stared at him for a few seconds before Cassie's voice broke through.

"Listen, don't go taking your frustrations out on me, Colm Kennedy. It's not my fault you haven't laid eyes on Siobhan since we got home. What happened to the 'stop worrying, it's just casual' speech you've been giving me for the last six weeks."

"Shut your gob, Cassie."

"You shut yours!"

Nanna crossed her arms and stared at the two of them as their father barrelled out. "What in the name of God is the racket out here? What's going on?"

"Nothing," Cassie said.

"Nothing," Colm said.

"Only two love sick fools, Brendan," Nanna said. "Nothing too serious."

"What are you on about, Mam?" Their father stood in the middle of the bar. He looked back and forth between his children with wide eyes.

"Well, it seems Cassie's found herself a fancy man in the Big Apple. And Colm here is sleeping with Siobhan."

"Sure, that's old news," Brendan said. "Been going on for years."

"What?" Cassie asked, seeing stars.

"Ah Jesus, Da, what did you have to go and do that for?" Colm raked his hand through his hair before turning to pull another pint.

"Why can't anyone ever tell me the truth?" Cassie threw one hand up in the air, guarding the wounded one close to her side. "You know what? I don't care. You and Siobhan were made for each other. But don't land me in the middle of your drama when it all goes to shite." She grabbed her coat just as she heard Mr. Kelly's lilted voice.

"Listen young Colm. I might be past my best before date, but I'm well and truly clear on what a lesbian is. It's the term vegetarian I'm having trouble with," the old man said.

Cassie slammed the door of the pub behind her, swinging her body into it and wincing as her arm protested the sudden movement. She was home all of five minutes and already the town knew her business. It wouldn't be long before news of her misfortunes made their way through the local rumour mill. Kennedy's was a pub, but it might as well have been a hair salon the way news traveled. If she were in New York she could step outside her building onto the sidewalk and be swallowed up into a sea of anonymity like the city's other eight million inhabitants. But she wasn't. Breathe, Cassie, breathe. A walk would clear her mind. She knew just where to go. She rounded the cobblestoned corner and smacked straight into a chest.

"Cassie. You could have at least said goodbye before you left."

Yep, Kilkenny was way too small.

CHAPTER 18

"We do get these requests from time to time, Mr. Carter. But I'll admit this is the first time the Kilkenny Trust has ever permitted it," said the woman. "They are incredibly grateful for your generous donation. So, here you go. All yours for one night." She held the keys up, but just out of his reach. "They've been through the rules with you though, right?"

Dax nodded.

"And you're not having more than one person in here?"

"Just the one," he said.

"Okay." She smiled. "There's one more thing. I'll need you to sign this insurance waiver." She slid a piece of paper across the desk.

Dax signed on the dotted line and took the keys from her outstretched hand. He glanced at the woman's name tag. "Thanks, Eileen. You've made my day." He took the keys and followed the exit arrows back out to the atrium where Zander waited, nearly buzzing with excitement.

"Hang on, Zander. I need to text your sister and tell her it's all systems go."

It was going to take a couple of days to put it all together, but with the help of the hotel's concierge—whom he paid handsomely—Dax had rented the castle, hired a butler, a caterer and a decorator to make the evening at the castle a dream come true for Cassie. Getting permission from the trust to use the castle for a night was a hard sell. At first, the chair of the board had been adamant they couldn't help him, but the deeper he opened his pockets, the more willing she became. He even threw in some pro bono work and promised the woman that Crave would come up with a brilliant fundraising strategy for Kilkenny Castle. Finally, he'd poured his heart out to her and explained he was desperate to win back Cassie Kennedy. In the end, he didn't know if the chair was a shrewd business-woman or a hopeless romantic. Either way, he got what he wanted.

"You look pleased with yourself," Zander said. "That must be the key to the castle?"

"This, my friend, may in fact be the key to Cassie's heart."

"You're sure this is going to work?"

"I'm not sure of anything, but I'm going with my gut. Cassie told me her dream date is right here in this castle. Her favourite place on earth. And I'm about to make that happen."

"What makes you think she's going to want to spend it with you?"

"Well that's where the magic comes in. I need to convince her she does want to spend it with me."

"Good luck with that."

"Hey, who's side are you on, anyway?" Dax shoulder-butted Zander as they walked back to the parking lot. "Come on, I've got work to do."

Cassie spent two hours with Rhys in a café around the corner from Kennedy's Pub. It was the best conversation they'd had in years, including when she thought things were going okay in their relationship. He'd apologized repeatedly and at first was put off that she didn't seem as upset by the whole affair as he expected.

The thing is she believed she was as much to blame for things going wrong as he was for cheating on her. Since she'd been away from him and Kilkenny, she'd come to realize that she was more in love with the idea of being married and starting a family than she had been with Rhys himself. He said he'd been confused for a long time, but Cassie's leaving had brought him back to reality. He knew what he'd lost.

"Do you think we could try again, Cass?" He reached across the table and took her hand, the expression on his face hopeful.

"Rhys, I don't think you've listened to a word I've said."

"No, I have. But I couldn't forgive myself if I didn't try. You were the best thing that ever happened to me and I threw it away."

"You were in my car. On some level, you must have wanted to be caught. If it wasn't Amy, it would've been someone else." She smiled. "You weren't happy. You felt trapped. You don't know what you want out of life yet and I understand that now. You're only feeling this way because I've told you I have moved on and I love my life in New York City. But you'll get there."

"You've met someone, haven't you?"

"I have, yes. But it wasn't meant to be." Cassie's heart ached as her thoughts turned to Dax. "But he did help me get over what happened. I was broken when I met him," she hesitated. "You must admit your timing left a lot to be desired."

"I know. I'm so sorry. I can't apologize to you enough." Rhys's eyes misted over.

"I'm not saying it to get another apology from you, but it was hard for me. My self-respect was in tatters when I met Da—" she stopped. "Anyway, he gave that back to me and I'll never forget him for it, but we're at different stages in our lives. He has—" she gulped. "Other priorities right now."

"He's a fool if he doesn't see what I see in you."

"It's complicated." Her phone buzzed in her hand. A message from Siobhan flashed across the screen. "It's been great seeing you, but I have to go." She rose to her feet and he stood, facing her.

"You too. Take care of yourself." He hugged her lightly, her bandaged arm between them, and kissed her cheek. A civilized goodbye.

"I will." She walked to the door and turned back briefly. "Goodbye Rhys."

"Goodbye Cassie." His shoulders drooped and he turned away from her.

As she stepped outside she thought back to what Nanna Kit said. Okay, maybe she did get the revenge gene, after all. Rhys's apology had been genuine, but Cassie couldn't deny that a small part of her was a smidgeon happy that he'd realized what he lost, but she kept that to herself. As she walked back to the pub, she opened the message from Siobhan.

SO: Girl's night?

CK: Now you're talking. Where?

SO: Kilkenny Castle?

CK: Huh? Have you lost the plot woman?

SO: Nope. Meet you there 8:00? Wear something nice.

CK: What are you up to?

SO: It's a surprise.

CK: You know how I feel about your surprises. Historically, they don't usually work out that well for me…

SO: Do me a favour—forget about history tonight. Keep an open mind and think about the future. Can you do that?

CK. Okay. You win.

SO: See? Doesn't that feel good?

CK: I guess we'll find out.

SO: Oh, and don't eat.

~

Cassie stared in amazement at the hundreds of glass-shrouded candles that lined the walkway of Kilkenny Castle. The place held a lifetime of fond memories, but tonight all she remembered was the last night she spent with Dax. She'd told him all about working at Kilkenny Castle when she was younger. After that they ran through their lists of favourite foods, favourite colours and he made love to her until the wee hours of the morning. The perfect end to a perfect night.

She smiled and blinked back tears. No more Dax. It was over. She got it now. He was her rebound guy. Too bad she'd had to split her heart wide open, feel so much, and hurt so deep, all to start healing. Heal she would, but it was time to let Dax go in her heart and her head. She didn't have the emotional bandwidth required to go through this again. She pulled her coat up around her neck. The wind had a bite. She stared at the candles as she reached the castle entrance. Someone had sure gone to a lot of trouble. Cassie reached the entrance and raised her hand, but the heavy door opened.

A tall, grey-haired gentleman dressed in a black suit smiled. "Good evening, Miss Kennedy. Welcome to Kilkenny Castle. Please, come in." He stepped to the side, gesturing with his hand.

"Oh. Um, sure." She jerked her head back. *A butler?* She stepped inside and the familiarity of the place hit her.

"May I take your coat?" He smiled.

"Yes, well, you'll have to help me out of it first." The sling made it impossible to wear the garment properly.

"Of course. Allow me."

He plucked the coat off her shoulders easily and was gone. What had Siobhan gotten them into tonight? The last time a butler had greeted her at the door—no. She shook her head. Not going there. There was a huge difference between this butler and the one in Vegas. That had been like the set of *Eyes Wide Shut*. This was more like the set of *Downton Abbey*, complete with Carson. She shook her head and stifled a giggle. Siobhan was always full of surprises.

Cassie smoothed the front of her black boat-neck dress with her good hand. She wasn't sure what Siobhan had meant by her directive to dress nice. It was too quiet here for a party. She scanned the foyer, smiling. God, how she loved this place. She'd worked here for two years as a summer student and knew every nook and cranny. Heat crept up her neck and into her face as she thought about Dax again.

It had all started when he asked her to describe her ultimate dream date. She said she'd happily marry any man who could arrange a date at Kilkenny Castle. Later that night, she told him she'd changed her mind and he was her dream date and she didn't care where they went. She touched the back of her hand to her cheek now, chastising herself for conjuring up the once happy images.

"Follow me this way, Miss Kennedy." The butler reappeared and led her down a hallway.

"Is Siobhan O'Mara here? Or am I early?"

"You are right on time, Miss Kennedy.

She stepped inside the drawing room and gasped at the transformation. All the ropes and stanchions had been removed and for a place that had been vacant for over eighty years, it sure looked lived-in. A fire roared in the hearth and soft music played in the background of the cozy room. Her nose followed a delicious aroma to a table located near the windows, set elaborately for two. He fixed her a glass of red wine at a bar near the wall of windows.

"Where is everyone?" She accepted the glass from his outstretched hand.

"I believe you are the guest of honour, Miss Kennedy."

Cassie raised an eyebrow as she sipped. Good wine. She catalogued every detail of the room. It was just as she remembered. "What's going on here? I worked in this castle years ago and I'm sure there was a policy about private usage." She turned around and scanned the room, but he'd disappeared.

She should be nervous, but Siobhan wouldn't let anything happen to her, would she? She was fun-loving and a little impetuous, but she wasn't dangerous. Cassie walked over to the mantle and admired the old photographs there. She laid down her wine glass on a side table. If there was fire in the hearth and beverage-drinking on antique carpets, why not break all the rules and fondle the artifacts? She picked up a likeness of Lady Margaret

Butler and admired it when she noticed light footsteps on the carpet behind her.

"Tell me, how did the Trust's chair agree to let anyone use the castle for a private function? I worked here as a summer student one year and Fiona Butler wouldn't permit water bottles in this place. How did we get from there to private dinner parties?" She set the frame back in place and picked up her wine glass.

"Cassie."

The hair on her arms stood at attention and she nearly dropped the wine glass onto the antique carpet. With his megawatt smile and black suit, complete with tails, Dax was the picture of a nobleman. His eyes twinkled and her breath hitched. His expression darkened as his gaze landed on her bandaged arm, propped in a sling and resting along her side. He looked up again with a mix of pain and regret in his eyes.

"Dax."

"Hi." He stepped closer and placed a chaste kiss on her cheek.

"How?"

He nuzzled a few seconds longer and breathed her in.

Cassie's stomach flip-flopped as it always did whenever he was near. "What? I mean—" So many emotions flooded through her that she couldn't articulate.

"Welcome to Kilkenny Castle, m'lady." He stepped away and gestured around the room with his hand. "You once told me your ultimate dream date was right here. You said it was your favourite place on earth."

She'd said a few things that night. Her heart pounded as she took in the sight of him. This was impossible. A wall of tears mounted, but she couldn't cry. This was the single most thoughtful thing anyone had ever done for her.

"Why are you here?" Her voice barely worked. Damn her easily-wooed damsel whisper.

"You have to ask me that?" He cupped her cheek, caressing her skin.

"Dax." She closed her eyes and leaned into his hand. How she'd missed his touch. His thumb brushed along her bottom lip and a soft sigh escaped.

"Please, let me explain. I know it's confusing. And I'm sure Helen has left you with an impression of things that isn't exactly accurate."

She closed her eyes and groaned at the mention of the woman's name. "Why'd you have to bring her up?"

"Because she's responsible for much of this."

She started to protest, but he raised his hand. "And I'm responsible for the rest, I know that. Please hear me out. If I'd been honest with you, none of this would've happened."

"I like a man who takes responsibility for his actions, but honestly, it doesn't change a thing."

"You mean you won't hear me out?" His eyes clouded with disappointment.

"I will hear you out, but I have no intention of changing my mind." She laid her wine down on a side table before the inevitable happened and reached for Dax's hand. She guided them both to the red settee near the fireplace. "I can't believe we're sitting on this." She shook the thoughts away. "Never mind that. Helen is a nasty piece of work, I'll grant you that. But I think we can agree on one thing. She is devoted to her family."

"I can't argue with that. Though if you ask Vanessa and Zander they might tell you that devotion borders on insanity at times."

"Right. So, her delivery was designed for shock and awe." She lifted her left arm up as proof. "Which was successful." His face tightened. "But at least she was truthful with me."

"Are you sure about that?"

"Was the boy on the ice your son?"

He met her eyes and nodded.

"Right, so she may be a bitch, but she's a truthful one."

"Jury's out on that." His blue eyes turned a stormy grey. "What else did she tell you?"

"It doesn't matter. Don't you see? I saw you guys on the ice before Helen arrived. I didn't know it was you of course, you were too far away, but I saw you with him. I saw how he threw his arms around you. It was so—" She choked up. "It was the pure definition of love." A single tear rolled down her face and he caught it with his thumb.

"His name is Adam. He's eight and he's in a wheelchair, courtesy of his mother, but we don't talk about that." His expression hardened.

"What? How?" Cassie blinked back surprise.

"Drunk driving."

"My God. How can you stand to look at her?"

"Lucky for me I don't have to."

"But I saw you guys together. You and Vanessa and—" Cassie stopped.

He blew out a deep breath before his features relaxed. "I've been wondering all this time what Helen could have said to make you so upset that you'd almost cut your arm off to get out of there. She told you Vanessa is Adam's mother, didn't she?"

Cassie nodded.

"Christ, that woman would sell her soul to the devil to get what she wants." Dax slumped against the settee, a rigid line formed along his jaw line.

"Vanessa isn't his mother?" Cassie swallowed hard.

"Vanessa has been more of a mother to Adam than his own mother ever was. But no, she's not. My ex-wife, Marley Carter, is his mother."

"Where is she?"

"Probably dead in a ditch somewhere, if there's any justice in this world." He smirked in disgust.

Cassie's hand covered her mouth. "Why would Helen lie to me?"

"That's a long story. I promise I'll tell you everything. But first I need to tell you some other things."

"Okay." She steeled herself. If that was the first revelation, what the hell else did he have to say?

"I didn't tell you about Adam and that's on me. His condition is life-threatening and his care is all-consuming. When I first met you in Las Vegas, I knew there was something special about you. I knew you were a keeper, but I was so used to not letting anybody into our lives anymore. It's complicated. I learned early on that most women didn't want anything to do with Adam. So, I stopped making it an option. I closed myself off to the possibility of ever having anyone seriously in my life. He's a pretty big investment."

"He's a child. Who wouldn't want to get to know a child?"

"You'd be surprised. I wanted to let you in. I was this close." He used his thumb and forefinger to show her. "That morning at your place I was going to tell you all about him. Arrange a visit. Somewhere nice, the aquarium, something fun and see how it went. I knew he'd adore you." He grabbed her hand and held it. "Like father, like son."

"I was so mean to you that morning. I found out my brother and Siobhan were sleeping together and I lashed out. I was so terrible."

"You were upset, I get it. The phone call was from Vanessa. She was on her way to the hospital with Adam. Because of the nature of his spinal cord injury he is prone to episodes of autonomic dysreflexia, which can be life threatening. It's complicated, but if he gets any kind of infection and his body temperature spikes he'll have seizures. He gets a lot of urinary tract infections because of the injury and has catheters put in from time to time. As soon as his symptoms start we get him to the hospital. His doctor is an amazing woman."

"Oh, my God." The faraway look in his eyes made her want to take him in her arms and never let go. Her harsh judgements had been so unfair.

"You'd think I'd be used to it by now, but you never get used to it. Every time he goes in I'm conscious it could be the last time." His voice hitched and he moved closer to her. "When it happens, I drop everything—everybody—and go to him. It doesn't matter." He looked her square in the eye. "You understand?"

"Of course, I understand."

"Then you came along and made me feel alive again, but it wasn't fair to bring you into this when I couldn't guarantee I wouldn't have to drop you at any moment to be at Adam's side. I thought it'd be best to let you go before I got in too deep."

Cassie nodded. The tears fell freely.

"The problem is my head couldn't forget you. I couldn't pretend you weren't out there. My lips couldn't forget your kisses. My hands couldn't forget how you feel."

She wiped the wetness from his face.

"My heart couldn't forget that I had fallen in love with you."

Cassie sealed his lips with hers, swallowing his words as if hanging onto them to make them more real. His arms came around her and pulled her tight against him. His hands worked into her hair and she groaned into his mouth.

She pulled away. "Wait, where is Adam now? How could you have left him? What if something happens?"

"Adam is fine. Vanessa is with him and so is his doctor." He leaned in and kissed her again, but she broke it off in a matter of seconds.

"I'm serious, Dax!" She stood. "You need to go."

"What about your night here? This is your dream date."

"I don't care about the castle. I told you the last night we were together—you're my dream date. We need to go home."

He stood up and reached for her hand. "We?" His voice trembled.

"Yes! I could never forgive myself if something happened to him and you were here with me. Let's go home and you can be closer to him."

"My God woman, I didn't think there was any way to love you any more than I already did." He pulled her in to his arms and claimed her mouth like he'd never done before.

When they came up for air, Dax sat them both on the settee. "Just so you don't cut me off again and insist we leave this castle before my time is officially up here. Adam is fine. He's five minutes away at the hotel with Vanessa and her partner, Stephanie, who also happens to be his neurologist."

Cassie raised her finger. "Right. About Stephanie. You sent her to the hospital to operate on me?" Her eyes widened.

"What else was I going to do? When Siobhan called—"

"Siobhan called you?"

"Well, she called Zander, but he called me right away. I was already feeling sorry for myself, knowing I had lost you to Victor Ramirez, but when Zander told me what happened, I was beside myself with worry. I knew I could help and I'm not going to apologize for that, Cassie."

"I'm not asking you too." She smiled. "It's kind of sweet." A look crossed her face. "Wait, let me guess. My contract didn't include extended health benefits and full salary until I returned to work, did it?"

He held his hand up. "Well, no. Not exactly. But before you say anything about that, I believe Helen Roberts owes you that much. For pain and suffering." He pointed at her arm and she laughed.

"Fair enough, I can accept that."

"When I saw Victor in your office that day, I knew by the look on his face that he was interested in you. What I didn't know was whether he pursued you all on his own or if Helen had put him up to it."

"Gee thanks. You don't think I can get a man all by myself?" she teased.

"Oh, sweet girl, I know you can get a man all by yourself. You got me the moment you pretended you had an urgent phone call in Las Vegas just to get away from me." He kissed her forehead.

"You knew I didn't have a phone call?" She bit the side of her lip, crinkling her nose.

"I was pretty sure." Her eyes fell and he lifted her chin. "Don't be embarrassed, it was cute." He chuckled.

"You made me nervous," she said.

"You made me want you."

The room heated up about thirty degrees and she inhaled a shallow breath. He brushed a lock of hair away that had fallen across her eyes.

"I do think Victor was acting alone, though." Cassie changed the subject. "Helen admitted she was happy that Victor had decided to ask me out."

"Knowing I'd lost you drove me mad, Cassie. I couldn't sleep. I didn't know what to do to get you back."

"Turns out you did." She gazed up at him as his arms wrapped around her.

"Come with me." Cassie led him out of the drawing room and up the grand staircase.

"We're not allowed upstairs," Dax said. "I signed a waiver. No open flame—apart from that fire in the fireplace, no food outside the main room, and no going upstairs. I wouldn't be surprised if they didn't have a fire crew stationed right outside." He laughed easily and his eyes twinkled.

Cassie's stomach fluttered. "How much money did you donate to use this place?"

"A fair bit."

"That's what I thought. Come on, we're going upstairs." She took his hand and they started up the staircase.

"There's one more thing." Dax stopped mid-step and pulled his hand away. She turned to him. "I may have promised Fiona Butler that Crave Marketing is taking on a fundraising campaign for the Kilkenny Trust."

"You're the boss." She grinned and grabbed his hand. "But let's talk about Fiona later." She led him down a hallway with signage indicating the area was prohibited and opened a door to a suite of rooms. "These were Lady Margaret Butler's rooms. My favourite place of all."

They stepped into the room and she closed the door behind them. She crossed the floor and opened another door. A four-poster canopy occupied the centre of the room. Cassie sat on the end of it and beckoned him over.

"Of all the lads I dated here in Kilkenny, not one of them could make this happen."

"That's because they were boys. I'm a man. A man who'd do anything for you Cassie from Kilkenny. This is just the beginning."

"Right now, all I want you to do is kiss me."

"Your wish is my command, beautiful, but in the interest of full disclosure—" he trailed kisses down her throat and Cassie groaned softly. "I'm going to do more than that."

"I'm counting on it." She pulled his face up to meet hers in a tender kiss.

"But, first thing's first," he said.

"What's that?"

"Let me help you out of that sling." His eyes twinkled with mischief.

CHAPTER 19

DAX SLID HIS HAND ALONG CASSIE'S LEG IN A POSSESSIVE gesture as he shifted the rental car into drive and headed southeast onto The Parade toward Castle Gardens.

"I can't believe I just made out like a teenager on Lady Margaret's bed in Kilkenny Castle." Cassie laughed, her hand rested on his just above her knee. She leaned forward, her eyes locked on the side mirror as the castle faded from view. "Thank you for arranging this. You'll never know what it meant to me."

"I'm sorry we had to leave, but I didn't want to risk breaking Lady M's bed and having Fiona Butler trample my good name throughout Kilkenny."

Cassie giggled and he took his eyes off the road for a moment to study her. His heart thudded at the adoring look in her beautiful green eyes. There'd never be another woman for him. Ever. He slid his hand under her dress and caressed her thigh. He toyed with the idea of pulling off the road to have her right here. It's not like he hadn't done it before. But not yet. There was still a lot to resolve. They had the whole night ahead of them and a sturdy bed at the Lyrath Estate Hotel, just a few minutes away.

"Besides, I plan on spending more time here," he said.

"Oh yeah, and why do you want to do that?" Cassie shuffled closer to lean against him.

"Because you're here." He flashed a smile.

"Well, that's wonderful, but as soon as this hand is healed I'm heading back."

"You are?" The car jerked as he reacted to her words.

"Of course. Kilkenny is my home. My family is here and my heart will always belong here. But I'm beginning to love New York too." She laced her fingers with his and kissed the back of his hand. "And maybe one of its residents."

"You're coming back?" The car came to an abrupt stop.

"You thought I had left for good?" She turned fully in the seat to face him. "Why? Because I was so heartbroken over you that I couldn't bear to come back?"

"Well, when you put it that way, it sounds a little self-centred." He chuckled. "But yeah, something like that."

She playfully swatted his shoulder. "Get over yourself, Dax from New York."

He leaned in and caught her chin. "It's you I'll never get over."

"I wouldn't want you to," Cassie whispered before he claimed her mouth in a soul-searching kiss.

He wasn't sure how long they stayed that way. He was vaguely aware that a few horns blared and engines revved as cars pulled around them, but his focus remained on the woman who responded to his every touch. It took everything in him to tear away from her and drive the short distance to the nearby hotel where he'd booked out several rooms to accommodate Adam, his motley crew of friends and supporters, and one additional room in particular. He'd held out hope for a blissful reunion with the woman he loved.

Cassie believed there was nothing between him and Vanessa now, but that didn't mean she hadn't been hurt deeply. The cut on her arm would heal and maybe there'd be a small scar. Helen's actions would leave a bigger mark. He also had much to sort when he got back to New York. He'd never leave Cassie vulnerable to the woman's wrath again. He was ready to extract himself from the Roberts's hold on him, but he had to be careful not to hurt Adam in the process.

There were a lot of details to sort before Cassie could fully integrate into his life. She also needed to know everything about Marley and how the Roberts family had come to his rescue and made it all go away. And there was Adam. Dax knew the boy would adore Cassie as much as he did, once given the opportunity to spend time with her. Cassie appeared very willing to accept Adam's condition and the restrictions it would always put on their lives.

Dax grabbed Cassie's hand and kissed it as they walked toward the hotel.

"Good evening Mr. Carter," said the doorman.

"Evening," Dax said.

Cassie was quiet as they stepped over the threshold of the Lyrath. She let go his hand and walked toward the grand wooden staircase with its crimson-carpeted stairs.

"Have you stayed here before?" Dax moved to stand next to her.

"No." She ran her hand along the freshly polished wooden railing. "But I spent a lot of time here before I moved to New York."

"Work?"

"Wedding planning."

"I'm sorry." He placed his hand on her back.

"Don't be." She turned to him, leaning against the wooden post. "If one positive thing has come from my return it's that I had a really great conversation with Rhys today." She ran her hand down his arm. "After all this time, I think we finally understand each other."

"I see." His jaw tightened.

She smiled. "Mr. Carter. You're looking awfully green. Is that jealousy I see on that handsome face?" She reached up to touch it, but he stopped her.

"Yes." He wrapped his arms around her and pulled her tight against him. "I don't want any other man to understand you." His kiss was rough and she gasped. Her hands slid along his neck, ruffling his hair. When they finally broke apart, Cassie's chest heaved and she licked her lips. Dax groaned. "Come on, we're taking this upstairs. Now." He placed his hand along her back and ushered her up the stairs.

She stayed in step with him as they hurried up two flights of carpeted stairs. He grabbed her hand and led her to the right. When they were well down the corridor, away from prying eyes, he surprised her by wrapping his hands around her waist. He pulled her against him and crushed her mouth with his. He spread her flush against the wall and Cassie squealed.

"Be gentle." She laughed.

He trailed kisses along her jaw and neck. His other hand slid over her swollen breasts, around and down her back. He cupped her ass and she hooked her leg around his thigh.

"Dax." Breathless, Cassie broke their embrace, her heart threatening to beat out of her chest.

"Jesus, Cassie. I need to get you in this room before I take you in the hallway." He lowered her hands and she slid her leg down and rested her high-heeled foot on the floor. She leaned against him and his erection pressed against her thigh. They locked eyes, his flooded with heat and desire. He stepped away and slipped the key card out of his pocket and into the door she hadn't realized they were standing beside.

As the key card buzzed, Dax turned the handle and opened the door, keeping it in place with his foot. Somehow, she found her wits and pushed off the wall. He pivoted and placed his hands around her waist, lifting her with ease as she linked her legs around his hips. Her good hand gripped his face as she kissed him with great urgency. He walked them through entrance. The only sound besides their breathing was the click of the door behind them as he lowered her to the bed.

~

She awoke with Dax curled into her, his arm tight around her waist, ensuring she wasn't going anywhere. She smiled, thinking of their night in Vegas. But the fates had brought them together, repeatedly, and that counted for something. She chuckled softly, not wanting to wake him.

"I seem to recall the first time I got you into bed you laughed at me too." He whispered in her ear, squeezing her tight.

"You're awake." She turned over and brought her hand to his face. He kissed her longingly like they hadn't been wrapped in each other's arms for hours.

"I was laughing because you're holding me like you're expecting me to make a run for it. It made me think of that night in Vegas."

"Yes, well, I wasn't taking any chances."

"I think it's safe to say those days are done."

"I hope so." His finger trailed down her shoulder and back up in a repetitive motion.

"I know so." She drew circles along his smooth chest. "Earth to Dax. What's going on in that handsome head of yours?"

His brow knit and he pulled away from her. "I need to tell you everything. The Roberts. What they did for me. I need you to understand why I'm so deeply indebted to them and why I've let this thing with Vanessa get so out of hand." He pulled himself up into a sitting position and leaned against the headboard. "I feel like we can't go any further until you know everything. Just in case you—"

"I what?"

"Change your mind."

"About being with you?"

He nodded.

"That's not going to happen. But if it helps you to tell me everything, I'll listen." She sat up and turned to face him, pulling the sheet with her. Sensing his serious shift, she didn't try to touch him. Instead she let him start his story.

"We had a hard time getting pregnant. Marley had three miscarriages before we had Adam and two after. It took its toll on her. I said no more. I was through with the emotional roller coaster we were on and I couldn't watch what it was doing to her. Every time we lost another baby, another piece of her died." His voice wavered. "But the one who was really suffering was Adam." He blew out a long breath, as if pacing himself through the pain. "Her recovery period was longer each time. Not physically, but mentally. She'd slip into a severe depression and withdraw from Adam more and more. It got to the point that I couldn't leave her alone with him because I didn't know if she even had the wherewithal to get out of bed and tend to his needs." He drew his legs up and leaned forward, resting his arms on them, head bowed.

"I made excuses about fancy pre-schools and learning programs, which meant nothing to me. She'd always said she wanted to be a stay at home mom and I was happy with her decision. I was content to tend to the sea of laundry and the sink overflowing with dishes at night if Adam was happy and well-cared for. The thing is she knew that *I knew* she was no longer capable of being a mother to him. That's when the drinking started. Then the drugs. Prescription at first. Then harder street drugs."

Cassie reached out and took his hand, rubbing it. Her eyes never left his face.

"Adam left with me every morning and I brought him home every night," Dax said, never breaking the rhythm. "Sometimes she was passed out in the living room or at the table. Sometimes she was just gone. She'd disappear for days on end. I tried to get her help. She went to rehab a couple of times. Nothing worked. By this time, we hadn't slept together in over a year. I couldn't. Things were bad enough as they were, but I couldn't risk her getting pregnant again. She became more irrational and accused me of cheating on her." He shook his head. "I had plenty of opportunities, but the one thing I never did was cheat on her. I cursed her and on some level I even despised her. But I never cheated on her. I realized she wasn't going to get better and I had to let the guilt go and get out for Adam's sake."

"Of course, you did. Because you're a wonderful father." Cassie scooted closer, leaning against him, supporting him.

He barked a bitter laugh. "A wonderful father wouldn't have fallen for Marley's assurances that she was better. A wonderful father wouldn't have let her anywhere near

Adam, let alone allow her behind the wheel of a car with him. If I hadn't been so stupid, Adam wouldn't be in this situation." He put his head in his hands.

"You can't blame yourself for Marley's actions. They're hers to live with for the rest of her life."

"Marley doesn't even know if she's in this world. She doesn't feel pain anymore. How's that for justice? It's Adam who feels pain, every day of his life. And I watch him. Every day of *my life*. Wishing I could take it all away. Wishing it was me instead."

She couldn't help thinking he didn't have to wish. Dax was living his own version of pain. Guilt could cut deeper than an ice skate any day of the week.

"The irony was the day it happened, I was meeting with Zander. He was my closest friend since college and he knew things were bad with Marley, but he didn't know it all. I told him everything and he never hesitated. We planned to leave that night. I was going to take Adam and get on Franklin's plane and head to New York to start over. I was an hour too late. And I will never forgive myself for that."

Eventually, Cassie lay back in his arms. Dax stopped a few times to work through his grief. He explained how Zander and Franklin had shown up at the hospital the night of the accident. Zander had confided the situation to his father, a man who was accustomed to fixing everything with his money, and they did just that.

Cassie listened carefully to every word. It was an unbelievable story, but she could tell by the level of his grief every bit was true. In Marley's drunken, drug-induced haze, she had fled the accident scene. She'd left Adam strapped in his car seat, not knowing if the child was alive or dead. Franklin had a private investigator track her down, sober her up and get her to the police station. The report states she didn't remember leaving the scene and woke up later in a nearby alley. A doctor, arranged by Franklin's people, had explained to police that Marley had been suffering severe postpartum depression and blacked out due to her medication. The accident had caused some minor head trauma, which had impaired her judgement. It had all been declared one big tragic accident because what mother would harm her child willingly like that?

The pain he carried every day was hard for Cassie to comprehend. On top of it all, he'd let Marley go without punishment because it was best for Adam. Most people wouldn't do that. Their thirst for revenge would cloud everything else. Dax didn't want any headlines about the accident, painting Marley as a drunk driver, nor did he want her to go to jail. Dax explained that Franklin's lawyers drew up an agreement and Marley signed it, forfeiting any parental rights to Adam in exchange for the assurance that Dax or Adam would never lay eyes on her again. From that point on, they had become part of the Roberts clan in every way, but name. They were the family and support system Dax had always wanted, but never had.

He'd been an only child and his parents had died in a car accident when Dax was eighteen. They'd left him some money in a trust and he used it to go to Harvard—where he met Zander. With everything that had happened, the Roberts had taken Dax and Adam in and treated them like their own. It all made much more sense now. Cassie could never promise to like Mrs. Roberts, but she did understand the woman's claim on them. She also understood why the woman wanted Vanessa to spend her life with this man.

Cassie lay in Dax's arms, listening to his even breathing until she was sure he'd fallen asleep. She slipped from his arms and grabbed her phone on the bed night stand. It was half seven. She opened her messages and fired off a text to Siobhan.

CK: Helping the enemy I see.

SO: Someone needs to help you get your love life back on track.

CK Who said I needed help with my love life?

SO: You need all the help you can get. Besides it keeps you the fuck out of mine. Speaking of which, Colm's not speaking to me. You have anything to do with that?

CK: Nope.

SO. Liar. Liar. Your drawers are on fire. Or if the night went as lover boy planned, they're hanging from the lamp.

Cassie grinned at the phone.

CK: I need your help.

SO: What?

CK: My turn for a surprise.

SO: Can't you two just get married and buy the house with the white picket fence and be done with it?

CK: Oh, come on. After all the help you gave Dax, it's been enlightening, Shi. You're a real romantic at heart. I never knew.

SO: I am not. Just couldn't bear another six months of your moping.

CK: Meet me downstairs in the dining room at Lyrath Hotel in half an hour.

CHAPTER 20

"Should I be nervous that you insisted on driving? I'm really at your mercy since I have no idea where we are." He chuckled. "Are you taking me to some Celtic ruins where you can have your way with me on New Year's Eve?" He wagged his eyebrows and shot her a playful smile.

Cassie laughed. "I think what we've been doing for the last twelve hours sufficiently falls under the label of having my way with you."

"And I'll never get tired of it." He leaned close, kissing her neck, taking his time in the dip near her shoulder, driving her wild. "Though, I hope it classifies much higher than sufficient." He whispered in her ear.

A soft sound escaped her lips and she was unable to make eye contact for fear of driving off the road. Oh, what this man did to her.

"Where are you really taking me anyway?" Even though they hadn't had much sleep, Dax looked somewhat rested, and much more at ease. His hand rested on her leg.

"Home." Cassie shot him a brilliant smile and

manoeuvred the rental car through Kilkenny City until they reached St. Kieran's Street, the home of Kennedy's Pub and Inn. She pulled into the lot behind her childhood home and family business and looked at Dax.

"Well, it's not as sophisticated as the Big Apple, but this is it."

Dax took his time getting out of the car, sizing up the stone structure. "Wow, Cassie this is amazing."

"It'll do."

"It must be centuries old." He held Cassie's hand as they crossed the lot. The faint sound of Irish music wafted into the air.

"Thirteenth century."

"Amazing." His eyes raked over every crevice of the stone structure and he ran his hand along the wall.

"I didn't take you for much of a history buff." She was genuinely surprised as appreciation danced across his face.

"I'm not just a pretty face you know," he teased.

"I do know that."

"Or just a brilliant business mind." He narrowed his eyes.

"All right, now you're showing off." She smacked him in the chest, and he caught her by the arm and pulled her close.

"I did a few history courses as electives in college. It fascinated me. Being here makes me appreciate the power of the Old World versus the New World. North America is but a baby compared to Ireland."

She stared into those blue eyes that had reeled her in only two months ago, realizing there was so much about this man she couldn't wait to get to know.

"Adam has got to see this place. He'd love it."

"Yeah?"

"Definitely. That is unless—"

"Unless what?"

"Unless you want to wait. Is it too soon to thrust him into your life? You can be honest with me."

"Dax, Adam is your son. He's an extension of you. You and I are together and I'm not going anywhere so that means Adam is going to be a part of my life too."

Dax swept her into his arms, kissing her breathless. When they finally pulled apart she said, "You ready to meet everyone?" He nodded, kissing her one more time before she swatted him away, laughing.

"Me too," she said. "Come on." She grabbed his hand and pulled him around the corner before he had a chance to ask her what she meant. A crowd of smokers had gathered outside the front door. Pints of Guinness and Smithwick's, the local favourite, lined the outdoor tables in front of Kennedy's, waiting to be guzzled.

As they pushed through to the front door of the pub, a chorus of hellos sounded.

"There she is!"

"Welcome home, lass!"

"Aren't you a sight for sore eyes!"

All from the lips of long-time patrons and family friends. Once inside, she scanned the room. Her father and Colm commanded their posts, working each side of the bar and Nanna Kit was in the middle. All Cassie's brothers and sisters were here tonight, not only because it was the hottest ticket in town to ring in the New Year, but also because they'll be working their feet off on one of the busiest nights of the year. Nanna Kit had given Cassie a pass, but only because of her arm, not because she was bringing her new boyfriend along. As her siblings well knew, if you were dating one of the Kennedys, there was no such thing as a free pint. No money exchanged hands, but you damn well worked for it waiting tables or cleaning up. Your pick.

Nanna Kit caught her eye. "There you are, my girl." She beckoned Cassie to the bar. She nodded in Dax's direction. "Looks like you got it all sorted out."

Cassie smiled. "Yes, Nanna. Everything is fine."

"I guess that's why you never came home last night or this morning."

"Nanna." The heat crept to Cassie's face.

"All right, let me see this lad."

Cassie reached behind her and pulled Dax's hand, trying to edge him into a spot next to her at the bar. "Dax, this is my grandmother, Kathleen Kennedy."

"Nice to meet you Mrs. Kennedy." Dax took her hand and flashed her a dazzling smile.

She stared at him for a moment not speaking. Cassie's heart thumped in her chest. Nanna Kit eyed him up and down. "Well, I can certainly see why you didn't come home last night. Or this morning. I wouldn't have either."

"Nanna!"

Dax laughed and Nanna Kit came around to the other side of the bar and gave Dax a proper welcoming hug. He winked at Cassie.

"Hello there. I'm Brendan, Cassie's father. You must be Dax. Welcome to Kennedys." Her father waltzed by carrying a tray of empty glasses in one hand and spun his mother around to the music with the other as he headed back to his post. "We'll have a pint before the night is over," he called over his shoulder. "But right now, I'm up against it. I'll be back." He was swarmed the minute he stepped behind the bar.

"Is it always like this in here?" Dax stared at the two women as he took in the bar's surroundings. The place was well and truly on bust.

"Yes," they said in unison.

Nanna Kit gave Cassie a knowing look and pointed through the crowd.

"Come on," Cassie said, barely able to contain her excitement. "I've got a surprise for you." She took Dax's hand and steered him through the crowd.

"Wait a minute—is that?" Dax stopped mid-stride. At a corner table, not far from where the live band performed on stage, sat Zander, Siobhan, Vanessa, and Stephanie all laughing and smiling. At the end of the table, a very excited Adam was propped in his wheel chair. Cassie's brother Braden sat next to Adam, holding a bodhran, while Adam tried to hit the Celtic drum as best he could.

Braden's eyes met Cassie's and she mouthed the words thank you and touched her heart with her hand. He winked at her and cocked his head.

"You're not the only one with tricks up your sleeve." She strained on her tip toes to whisper in his ear.

Dax turned to her with wet eyes. "What did I ever do to deserve you?"

Before she answered he pulled her into his arms and claimed her lips. When they broke apart he took her face in his hands. "I love you. You know that, right?"

She nodded, tears brimming. "And I love you."

"Come meet my son."

"With pleasure."

~

Over the course of the night, Zander edged closer to Siobhan. Cassie stole a glance or two in Colm's direction. He was busy, but not so busy he didn't notice Zander all over Siobhan. Colm was doing his best to look nonchalant, but Cassie caught his daggers once or twice. She could tell by the cut of his jaw he was pissed, but she also knew he wouldn't do anything about it tonight. And not here.

"Hello." Cassie wormed into a space at the bar between old Mr. Kelly and a young girl, who was too young to be garnering the attention she was getting from her push-up bra and mini dress, and working too hard to catch Colm's eye.

"You having something?" Colm nodded at Cassie.

"How are you?"

"Hundred percent. What'll you have?"

"Colm."

"Cass, don't." He met her eyes and there was genuine hurt there.

"I'll have a glass of bubbly if there's one going around." Colm turned around to open the cooler door and retrieve the champagne.

"Good evening to you, Miss Cassie. You're a lovely addition to the bar," Mr. Kelly said. "Really classes up the joint." He leaned back on his stool and shot a side-glance at the young girl to Cassie's right, raising his eyebrows in a knowing look.

"Good evening, Mr. Kelly. And how are you faring tonight, sir?" she asked.

"Fair to middlin' I suppose. Ready to ring in a new year. And how about yourself?"

She turned around, her back leaning against the bar, her eyes seeking out the table across the room where Dax and Adam sat with the rest of the crew. A New Year and what would it bring? She mused, watching these new people in her life mixing with the old people in her life. "Yes, I think I'm ready for a new year with new beginnings. I'm ready to try new things." She shot the old man a smile over her shoulder.

"Never too late to open the mind and the heart up. To

try new things. Even at my age." The old man pivoted on his stool to follow Cassie's gaze.

Cassie smiled, watching Dax and Adam interact. Her heart swelled at their happiness. She knew from Dax it wasn't going to be smooth sailing all the time. It never would be. But they'd take what they could get, be joyful when things were good, and she'd support him when things weren't.

As her gaze wandered to Zander and Siobhan, she crossed her arms. They were all over each other and would be better off getting a room. But what really caught her attention was Vanessa and Stephanie huddled together, oblivious to anyone else in the room. The way the two looked at each other—their steady eye contact. A quick brush of their hands. There was a quiet understanding between them. Nothing to prove. It was heart-warming.

"You have any New Year's resolutions, Mr. Kelly?" Cassie asked, her eyes still on the two women.

"In fact, I do. I'm going to be more open-minded about things."

"Oh yeah? Like what?" The old man followed her gaze to the women in the corner.

"Vegetarians, for starters. I'm going to be more tolerant of vegetarians."

Cassie turned towards the man and burst out laughing, shaking her head.

She turned back to the bar to find her champagne waiting for her, but Colm was not. Cassie rejoined the table, which became a revolving door for family and friends—the genuinely interested and the mildly curious—to meet Dax and the others. Everyone looked for signs that Adam was crashing from exhaustion, but with the time change, mixed with the excitement, the boy was hanging on just fine. When the band played a slow number, Cassie and Dax wheeled Adam onto the dance floor. The pleasure on the little boy's face was intoxicating as they spun him in circles.

Cassie's thoughts returned to the ice rink at Rockefeller Centre a few short weeks ago. This time her heart was full of love and hope. Adam's adoration for his father was pure. The little boy, who should have nothing but skepticism for everyone and everything, had a heart as big as the sun and just as warm. He smiled at Cassie and she melted. As the music stopped and the band counted down from ten to the midnight hour, Dax reached for her.

"Happy New Year, Dax."

"You've already made my year, Cassie." He enveloped her and she wrapped her good arm around his neck, swaying as she stared into his blue eyes. His lips kissed away all the pain of the last year and held the promise of something exciting and new.

THE END

ABOUT THE AUTHOR

The Keeping Kind is Kallie Clarke's debut novel in The Kilkenny Chronicles—a new contemporary romance series. Kallie is the alter ego of historical romance author Melanie Martin. Kallie has an MA in history and lives in St. John's, NL Canada. When not reading or writing she is spending time with her twin girls, her husband, their dog, and her large extended family of Irish descent.

READ MORE

Black Ink Romance is proud to publish *The Keeping Kind* by Kallie Clarke. If you would like to join our review team for an opportunity to receive Advance Reader Copies of upcoming books please click here to sign up.

This is Kallie Clarke's debut novel. Her alter ego is historical fiction author, Melanie Martin. Check out her novel A Splendid Boy.

A Royal Newfoundland Regiment Love Story

In the summer of 1914, Daniel Beresford's innocent love affair with the merchant's daughter is discovered, forcing him to make an impossible decision to save his family from financial ruin. When news of the First World War reaches Middle Tickle, Daniel, who is torn between his love for Emma Tavenor and his responsibility to his family, enlists in the Newfoundland Regiment and departs for training.

When Emma learns her father is to blame for Daniel's unexplained departure, she follows him to England, hoping they'll be reunited. Yet on the voyage, she discovers the regiment has been called up and is already engaged in battle. She realizes her only hope of finding Daniel is to join the Voluntary Aid Detachment and make her way to the Western Front.

In 1916, on the eve of the Battle of the Somme, Emma and Daniel are reunited for a single, impassioned night near Beaumont-Hamel. Can the love they share survive the barriers of class and the horrors of battle? Or are their lives fated to join what would later be called a lost generation?

Finalist for the 2017 Scéal Book Awards

Finalist for the 2017 RONE Awards

Runner Up in the Historical: Victorian – 20th Century category of the 2017 RONE Awards

PRAISE FOR A SPLENDID BOY

"A must read for historical lovers!"

InD'tale magazine

"'A Splendid Boy' features vivid characters, spot-on description and a wicked sense of dialogue."

Northeast Avalon Times

"This book is exceptional for its depictions of the hardships of war in both Gallipoli and in Northern France for the Battle of the Somme."

The Miramichi Reader

"The novel is human and involving."

The Telegram

"Rich in historic detail."

Atlantic Books Today

"Melanie Martin deftly blends history and fiction in this epic romance set against the panoramic backdrop of Newfoundland society torn by class struggle, the Great War, and the sacrifice of a generation of

young men on the battlefields of France, Belgium, and Gallipoli. A real page-turner. You will not be disappointed."

Frank Gogos, Author of The Royal Newfoundland Regiment in the Great War

"Prepare to be swept back in time. Melanie Martin has a gift for bringing history to life in a story that's as remarkable as it is sensual. This spellbinding tale is what happens when a historian has a natural talent for storytelling. From the rugged coast of Newfoundland to the tragic fields of France, Daniel and Emma's journey will leave you breathless."

Victoria Barbour, USA TODAY Bestselling Author

"This book would make a fantastic movie for many reasons. War. Battle. Romance. Suspense. All great elements of a good story. And the characters are strong—the reader connects to both Emma and Daniel and genuinely wants to see them thrive."

Edwards Book Club

"A Splendid Boy is a treasure of engaging history and incredible love. Well done, Melanie Martin."

Books & Benches blog

"Martin's story is heartfelt."

Historical Novels Review

ACKNOWLEDGMENTS

This was an experiment in every sense. I wrote the majority of this book in November 2017, during Nanowrimo or National Novel Writing Month. A lot of obstacles cropped up—a business trip, a spur of the moment family trip, some minor sickness, and a hefty time change that was almost my undoing on the last day, but I set a goal and went for it. There were days I got up at five am to get my word count in before work. There were days when no matter what I did, the words wouldn't come. There were days I aimed for 2K and got 5K. Setting out to complete a full draft of a manuscript in thirty days was one of the most challenging goals I'd ever set for myself. Never underestimate your abilities when you want something bad enough.

Thanks to my amazing family, who willingly occupied my children when I needed to write during the day (with a clear head) and not ten o'clock at night when I was long past being able to think coherently. My mom did yeoman's service on November 30th—when the big push was on and I had 8,200 words left to get. We'd just flown three quarters of the way across the country to visit my brother's family and she occupied four children all day so I could write my way to the finish line! She has always encouraged me to follow my heart and whatever crazy whim passes through it. Thank you mom! And my dad…who watches over all of us.

A big thank you to my husband, who must be sick of seeing my head stuck in a computer or a book by now, but never says so. All I ever seem to say is I'm almost done… and never am. And my beautiful girls, who don't quite understand what I'm doing, but love for me to take breaks so they can type their names on the computer in big bold letters.

Another big thanks goes out to my my cousin Mari-Lynne (aka Doc McStuffins to my children) for allowing me to dramatize her medical expertise!

I'm blessed with a big circle of friends and family whose support is unending. Thank you to my beta readers and biggest supporters always: April Traverse, Renee Ryan, Debbie Robbins, Victoria Barbour, Louise Henry, Debbie Marnell, Tara Martin, Jacinta Sinnott, Mari-Lynne Sinnott, Stephanie Sinnott, Theresa Sullivan, and Denise Snow. Your enthusiasm means so much to me!

And finally, to the ladies of Black Ink Romance—we have something special. Thanks for all your support and hard work and keeping me on the straight and narrow. I treasure our partnership always.